IMPOSTER SYNDROME

A GRIPPING PSYCHOLOGICAL THRILLER

ALAN PETERSEN

Copyright © 2024 by Alan Petersen

All rights reserved.

IMPOSTER SYNDROME is a work of fiction. Names, characters, places, images, and incidents are products of the author's imagination or are used fictitiously. Any resemblance to actual persons, living or dead, events, or locales is entirely coincidental.

No part of this book may be reproduced in any form or by any electronic or mechanical means, including information storage and retrieval systems, without the author's written permission, except for the use of brief quotations in a book review.

For permissions beyond the scope of this notice, please send your request to:

                contact@alanpetersen.com

JOIN ME

Want to be the first to get exclusive insights into my books, hear the latest news, and enjoy sneak peeks and more? Join my newsletter!

It's easy! Just sign up at www.alanpetersen.com/signup

ONE
MICHAEL

San Francisco's Billionaires' Row was where old money and tech execs collided. I wasn't in either of those two camps. I made my money by killing and putting people in danger — on paper, of course. After eighteen bestsellers, and with more than eighty million books sold, I had made it to the top of the thriller-genre publishing world, which afforded me the luxury of living amongst the bon vivants of the city.

All I ever wanted was to make a living writing. I never dreamed I could afford a home in this type of a swanky hood. Every time I looked out my living room window and saw the panoramic views of the San Francisco Bay — from the Golden Gate to the Bay Bridge — I was reminded that dreams can come true.

Billionaires' Row was an enclave of ultra-luxury real estate in the Pacific Heights neighborhood, one of the few that survived the 1906 earthquake.

I lived in a Victorian mansion, yet I spent most of my time in the detached mother-in-law suite on the property that I'd converted into my writing office. I would joke that it was like my very own Fortress of Solitude. My office was located about fifty feet from the main house. I had black out shades installed on the windows to remove the temptation to look out onto the bay. And I removed the phone line and ethernet cable to avoid those distractions as well.

My writing computer was bare bones, with just Microsoft Word installed. If I needed to check email or a fast internet connection to do research, I would go into my wired office inside the main house.

Here all I could really do was write. I know that it sounds extreme, but it was part of the process that had helped me write all my bestselling thriller novels. With millions of copies of my books sold worldwide and my novels translated into forty-five languages, there was no denying that my system worked, so I stuck to it.

That at least was the case until three months ago, when seemingly my well of words dried up, and my carefully designed writing sanctuary morphed into a custom-made prison cell where I sat for hours at my desk staring at a blank document on my computer screen.

I sat there with my hands on my desk, my head tilted back into the headrest of my chair, my gaze drifting off towards the wall to my right that showcased the fruits of my labor. Eighteen framed book covers, each a bestseller, each a testament to years of dedication. The last fifteen of them were written right here in this room. *The Midnight Hour*, my debut novel, held a place of honor, its cover a contrast of black and red that had once seemed so striking. Next to it was *Broken Silence*, the psychological thriller that had made me a household name. And then there was *Whispers in the Dark*, the crown jewel of my career, the book that had shattered sales records and turned me into a literary sensation. I had often caught myself gazing at these covers, drawing strength from them. But now they seemed to mock me, silent reminders that my wild and lucrative literary career was over.

On the shelf behind me sat three trophies, each sent to me by my publisher to celebrate the milestones of my career. The first was a sleek silver statuette that looked like an Emmy award; it commemorated the sale of one million copies. The second was a more ornate and golden trophy for selling ten million books. The most recent one gleamed with an almost surreal brilliance that celebrated fifty million books sold. As I approached the 100-million mark, I wondered what the publisher would send me. Now I was not sure I'd reach that milestone.

I had been sitting there like a damned fool for about forty minutes, thinking about all that, when my mobile phone began to ring. Dammit, I forgot to put it into silent mode as I usually did in my writing office. Perhaps I did that on purpose, welcoming the distraction of not being able to write. I picked up the phone from my desk and glanced at the screen. It was my agent, Lydia Geller; I knew why she was calling me, but I took her call anyway.

"Michael, it's me." Lydia's voice came through, tinged with a mix of concern and impatience. "I've been trying to reach you for days. We need to talk about the book."

"I know, Lydia," I said, my tone flat. "I'm working on it."

"You've been saying that for weeks now," she replied, showing a hint of frustration. "Michael, we've missed one deadline already. The publisher is getting anxious. They've invested heavily in this book and have it slated for release this winter — they need to see something to know that you're making progress."

"I'm aware of that, Lydia," I said, upset. Does she think I'm an idiot?

This wasn't for my first rodeo in this business.

"You haven't missed a deadline in fifteen years. If there is something going on, talk to me. You know you can trust me."

I stared at the blinking cursor on the blank page. There was nothing she could do, but leave me alone.

"I just need more time," I said, more to myself than to her.

"More time is something we don't have." Before I could say anything, I heard her sigh, and she said, "Look, I know how hard this is for you. But you always deliver. So get back at it. I know you'll break loose of whatever it is that is holding you back. But we can't afford another delay."

It seemed that she was pleading with me now, more than anything.

"I'm not a circus elephant ready to perform at the crack of the trainer's whip," I snapped back.

"Michael, you're one of the best writers in the world. I know you can do this. You've done it before. Just... find a way to push through. Okay?"

I heard another of her phones buzzing in the background. "I have to take another call. Just... Please, Michael. Try to get something out to me in a week. So I can show the publisher that you're back on track. We're running out of time."

Lydia hung up.

I felt relieved to be done with that conversation. Push through it? How dare she? I sat there for a minute stewing, but I calmed down because she was right. I needed to deliver. There must have been other times when I sat right in this chair, in front of that computer with deadlines looming and pressure mounting, and I always persevered. I did always push through. Right?

My phone buzzed. A text this time. I figured Lydia was sending me a "Ra-ra, you can do it" text as a follow up. I looked at the message, but it wasn't from Lydia. The caller's phone number wasn't displayed, instead the phone number came up as unknown and the caller ID was one word: Maybe.

Strange. Who could that be?
I read the message:

> Fraud

What the hell? This was my personal cell phone number. Very few people had it, so this must be someone I knew thinking they were being hilarious. They were not.

"I don't have time for this bullshit," I said out loud, ignoring the text. But the phone trilled again. Another message from Maybe:

> You're not who you think you are.

TWO
MICHAEL

Whoever had pulled this prank on me wasn't being funny. Their timing couldn't be worse with the struggles around writing the book. The person behind these text messages was pissing me off. I texted back.

> Not funny. Who is this?

I waited for a couple minutes but no reply. I got up and began to pace around my writing studio which now was more of my own self-made jail cell.

I stopped in front of the cover of *Whispers in the Dark*, remembering the thrill I felt when I had first conceived its story idea, the way the characters had leaped to life, demanding to have their stories told. I wrote that book in a fever, barely stopping to eat or sleep, so consumed was I by getting that story on paper. I wrote 110,000 words in two months.

I'd written less than 500 words in the past three months on this cursed project. And those words were trash. I was basically at zero words with the New York publisher chomping at the bit.

Those framed book covers had been a source of pride and motivation, now they laughed at me. Reminding me that in this business you were only as good as your last book, and I couldn't get the damned thing written.

What was wrong with me? Was my past success just dumb luck?

The cell phone buzzed again. I quickly made my way back to my desk and picked it up. A reply from Maybe.

> That's my life. Not yours.

My blood ran cold. What kind of sick joke was this?

I texted back:

> Who is this? How did you get this number?

I sat there with my arms tightly crossed over my chest as my eyes bore into my phone, waiting for a reply. I waited. And waited. Thirty minutes. But nothing.

I didn't know why I was letting this get to me. Perhaps since I was already feeling under the gun from my agent and publisher, the last thing I needed was someone else messing with my head.

And then there was Melody.

She wasn't helping when she began complaining about the state of our marriage. How I had changed these past few months. How I wasn't communicating with her anymore. That I was ignoring our eleven-year-old son, Dashiell. Sleeping on the pull-out couch in my studio versus at the house. Reminding me that we hadn't been intimate in the three months since I'd started to work on this damned book. It was the last thing I needed to deal with right now, so I snapped. I told her I didn't have time for her bullshit. That my books paid for our luxurious life, so she just needed to leave me alone until I was done with the book or get the hell out of my life. For two nights after that, I didn't hear a peep from Melody or from our son.

It was bliss not having to deal with her drama, but I still hadn't been able to write.

Yesterday I made my way to the main house for the first time since our fight and found she had moved out that same day. She'd left me a handwritten note on the kitchen counter:

> *I don't know what's going on with you, since you won't talk to me anymore, but you have changed. I would prefer being back in Modesto struggling to pay*

our bills with the man I fell in love with than living in this opulent home with the stranger you have become. Dash and I will be staying with my mother until you work things out. I hope it's not too late to save our marriage.

Well, that was a gut-punch. But I was surprised at how I felt about her leaving. I felt... relieved that she was gone. Out of my way. Maybe now I could get some work done.

So typical of her to say something like that. How happy we were when we struggled paycheck to paycheck. She was romanticizing being broke, which was easy to do from a multi-million dollar home.

I had always been proud of the life I had built from my writing. I grew up in Fresno in a working-class neighborhood. My parents struggled financially; my father turned wrenches as a mechanic for a living, my mom was a secretary, but it wasn't a horrible childhood. They tried their best. Since they couldn't afford to pay for my education, and I wasn't blessed with the athletic ability that earns college scholarships, I joined the National Guard strictly to pay for school. I wanted to write for as long as I could remember, but I knew that making a living as a writer was akin to winning the lottery, so I got a degree in English and became a high school teacher, all the while tapping away on my laptop on a novel while making slightly above minimum wage.

I met Melody during my sophomore year at Stanislaus State, a public university in Turlock. I went to that school because it was in my GI-bill budget, and the cost of living there was slightly better than in the ridiculously expensive state of California. Melody's parents were both college professors in Turlock. Although not wealthy, compared to my parents, they were downright rich in my eyes.

Melody was one smart cookie. She was accepted at Berkeley and graduated from there with honors. The only reason we met was because I took a class from her dad and she took my breath away when I saw her waiting for him outside of class one day.

I had always been an introvert, but I somehow mustered the courage to ask her out. After college, we married and settled into our regular semi-boring lives in Modesto, where I was amassing an impressive collection of rejection letters from agents and publishers. Melody worked in human resources for the City of Modesto. We both had decent, respectable jobs that would never get us out of Modesto and hoped that someday we would have been able to afford to buy a house out in the suburbs. We certainly couldn't have ever afforded to live in San Francisco back then.

But my writing finally paid off. Big time. More than we dared to ever dream. And we were living in luxury, and what does she do? She moves out of Pacific

Heights back to Modesto. The hell with her. I have a book to write.

I made my way back to my writing office.

Another text message from maybe:

> That wasn't your memory. You know that?

I looked out toward the bay feeling that whoever was messing with me via those text messages was watching me. It was mid-afternoon so the morning fog had burned off, and I could see the Golden Gate Bridge off to my right. A large container ship was making its way under the bridge toward the Golden Gate strait that led out to the Pacific Ocean heading out to a far away port out in the Pacific.

I couldn't see anyone. But as I stood there in my backyard halfway between the house and my office, I swore I heard someone's muffled screams.

It made me think of him. The imposter. There was no way that he could be heard from out here, could he? And I wondered: Was that the source of those text messages? It's not possible. There is no access to a smartphone there. This must all be in my head. I needed to get that part of my life behind me. I needed to write that book. That would set everything right.

I was about to go inside my office when my phone buzzed. I figured it was Melody, but it was the mysterious Maybe again.

> You're an imposter. That's why you can't write.

I looked around, more frantically that time. How could they know?

Part of me felt that I could go to him. He could get Lydia off my back. But another part of me refused to go there.

No. I didn't need his help. I can do this, I said to myself standing out there like Heathcliff hearing voices in the wind.

Almost immediately another text message arrived.

> No you can't.

THREE
CAPTIVE

I didn't know what my captor's endgame was. He had me chained up down here in an underground bunker, but for what purpose? At first I thought I was going to watch the gimp from *Pulp Fiction* pop out of a box. But nothing like that happened to me. Aside from when I was first attacked and kidnapped, my captor hadn't laid a finger on me. So then I began to think this was a ransom-type deal. But after this much time, I didn't think that was it either. Melody would have paid it by now. Even if they wanted a million dollars. That would have been no problem, and it wouldn't have taken long to get that money to pay the ransom.

But I'd been here a long time now. How long? I didn't know anymore. It hurt my head thinking about that since I was losing track of time; I had been down here for what felt like forever. Weeks had passed since I'd last seen my captor, that much I was certain of, which meant I'd been down here going on two months, maybe three.

Oh, God. *If this isn't about money. What does he want from me?* I looked around the bunker. It was one of those end-of-times shelters meant for the long haul. It was well-stocked with food and water, enough to last me at least a year. Was that this sick bastard's plan? Was he watching me as I ate through the supplies, drank all the water? Was he waiting until it was all gone? And then what? Would I slowly starve to death? Or die from dehydration with him watching? Getting his rocks off in such a depraved manner? I had scoured every inch of the bunker that my restraints allowed, looking for a way out, and I couldn't find a camera, but there had to be one hidden somewhere. Or was knowing that I was down here and would be here until I withered away and died all he needed to get his twisted needs met?

I could feel a panic attack coming on from these dark thoughts, so I had to calm my mind and steady my nerves. I had to find a way out of here.

The fear I felt when I woke here and when I last saw him had given way to despair. At first, I was certain he was going to kill me. But now? Not knowing what was going to happen to me was the worst part. I didn't know if it was night or day. And the isolation was maddening. This was something much more sinister and dark.

I screamed, knowing it was pointless; it was mostly

to release my anger and frustration over what was happening to me. When I wondered if I'd ever see my family again, I broke down and sobbed.

Part of me wished the sicko would just come down here and put me out of my misery.

FOUR
MELODY

Four days had passed since I'd taken Dash and driven east to Modesto, and Michael hadn't called or messaged me once. I felt like I didn't have any more tears to cry, but I was wrong. Was it something I did that made Michael stop loving me? Or had he been feeling this way for a long time, and I just didn't see it until it was too late?

Three months ago, everything was wonderful with our family. Or at least that was what I'd thought. How can twelve years of a happy marriage unravel so quickly? I'd racked my brains thinking about what could be happening. I didn't think there was another woman in the picture. He would have had to leave the house to have an affair. And he was usually in his studio writing, or with me and Dash. So what was it? How could he not even care that I'd moved out with our son? How could he not even check in once and ensure we'd made it safely to my mother's house? And as painful as it was that he didn't seem to care whether I might be alive or dead, the fact that he seemed to not care about our son either broke my heart into even more tiny little pieces.

Dash kept asking me when we were going home. And where was Dad? Looking into his sad and confused eyes when he asked about his father turned my sadness into anger. Michael could go ahead and neglect me. Toss our relationship into the garbage. But to be so cold and callous towards our son... What was wrong with him?

Tonight my two best friends from childhood came for a visit and they practically kidnapped me and took me to the Wet Spoon — a good old dive bar in Modesto that's been around since we were kids trying to sneak inside with fake IDs.

My mom was happy to watch Dash for a few hours so I could get my mind off my crumbling marriage. At first, I didn't want to go out. But as I sat on a hard chair in front of a wobbly table in a dimly lit bar, listening to 80s heavy metal from the speakers and the sound of billiard balls crashing and darts thudding into boards, I was glad I'd left the house. It didn't hurt that I was on my third Long Island Iced Tea.

I was just glad to be out with my dearest friends, Jessica and Taylor. The three of us have always had each other's backs, so it was not surprising they were ready to drive down to San Francisco to confront Michael for me.

"That asshole," Jessica said.

"Jess," Taylor said, trying to calm her down.

"No, I'm sorry — I know you love him, Mel, and he's the father of your child, but the way he's treating you. I'm sorry. He's an asshole!"

I felt Taylor look at me with concern. She must have been worried that I'd get mad and storm off. But Jessica was right.

"No need to apologize. You're right. He is being an asshole," I said as the three of us began to crack up.

I couldn't pretend that this girl's night out would wipe away my sadness, but it felt good to not feel so utterly sad every minute of the day. To instead feel boozy, lightheaded, silly. And angry. Angry at the way my husband of twelve years was treating me and our son.

"Do you think he's cheating on you?" Jessica asked.

"It crossed my mind when he stopped wanting to fuck me," I said, immediately feeling my cheeks flush with embarrassment over my booze-soaked, tawdry language.

All three of us burst out laughing, and when a couple of frat guys overheard and glanced over as if to signal, 'Maybe I can help with that problem,' we couldn't help but laugh even louder.

I've never cheated on Michael, and I'm not planning to, but I wouldn't lie: having these twenty-something good-looking guys at the bar giving me the look made this thirty-five-year-old mom, whose husband wouldn't even give her the time of day, feel good. I regained my composure and circled back to the question at hand.

"But seriously, no, I don't think Michael is having an affair. Not because he's still crazy in love with me, but because he's hardly left our property in months. Unless he's sneaking girls from Tinder into his writing studio without me knowing, I really don't think that's what's going on."

"But he always goes a bit crazy working long hours when he's writing a new book doesn't he?" Taylor said.

"Yes, but never like this. He's always treated it as a job. Monday through Friday from seven a.m. to five p.m. Then it's family time. Sure, sometimes he'll work longer hours or sneak into his office on a Saturday every now and then. But he always made time for me and Dash. Not with this project. He's just been holed up in that damned cottage he set up as his writing studio. And he won't come out. He even sleeps out there. Every time I try to talk to him, he looks away. He can't even make eye contact with me anymore. I think he suddenly hates me so much that he can't even look at me."

Dammit. I felt the tears welling up. The last thing I wanted to do was cry in a bar. Taylor and Jessica both reached out and they embraced me tightly.

"He doesn't hate you, hon. You said he's struggling

with this book, so maybe that's what's going on here, and he's not handling it well," Taylor said.

"That's for damned sure," Jessica added, making me smile.

"I don't know what to do," I said. "I've tried giving him space, but it's been four days now and not a word. Not even a text message. It's like he doesn't care about me. And okay, fine, maybe it's over between us, but to not give a damn about Dash? What the hell?"

"I say we drive down to the city and confront the asshole," Jessica said, grabbing the skewer from her almost-empty martini glass. "We storm the castle with our pitchforks and make him talk," she added, spearing the last olive with the skewer.

Taylor and I burst out laughing, which sure as hell beat crying into my pillow like I'd done the last few nights. But, realizing we were in no condition to drive anywhere, we ordered an Uber to take us home.

It was funny; even though I was in my mid-thirties, married, and had an eleven-year-old son, I felt like I was fifteen once again, trying to sneak home after blowing curfew. My mom just smiled as she watched me walk into the house tipsy.

"I'm glad you had a good night out, sweetheart. You deserved it."

"Thanks, Mom," I said as I hugged her.

She said goodnight and went to bed. She seemed so alone in the three years since my dad had died, and it made me think how alone I'd felt these past few months, though my husband was still there in my life, unlike my mom. But for how long? For the first time since Michael began to pull away from me, I began to think that my marriage might really be over.

How could I not have seen this happen? It was as if all of a sudden a switch had been turned on to change his feelings towards me. Towards Dash. And I remembered his agent, Lydia, had called me a few weeks ago when Michael missed a writing deadline for the first time in his career. Lydia told me that Michael seemed unable to write anymore, and that he had become distant and nasty towards her as well. I hadn't put much stock in it. Lydia was an agent, and part of her job description was to worry and fret over her clients. But Michael had always pulled through when it came to his work. Now, however, I thought back to our phone conversation.

"I'm sorry for prying like this, Melody, but are you guys having problems that could be affecting his work?"

"Everything was wonderful until recently, when he changed. He basically moved into his writing studio ignoring me and Dash. When I tried to talk to him about what was going on, he just got mad and stormed off. He told me I needed to stop bothering him since he was busy on the new book."

"That's terrible. I'm so sorry, Melody."

"I tried to be understanding and let him work. But now you said he missed a deadline. He's never done that. Did he send you the first few chapters like he always does?"

"No. He didn't do that either."

That didn't sound like him at all. I knew how Michael and Lydia worked. He was a discovery writer, so he wouldn't outline. But he would hand in the first few chapters to Lydia, who had worked as a developmental and acquisition editor for one of the Big Five Publishing houses before becoming a literary agent. She would offer advice over those early chapters. When Michael was fifty percent done with a manuscript, he would send that to Lydia until he was finished, then he would send her the rest of the manuscript. She would offer her editorial suggestions and he would do his rewrites, then Lydia would send that off to the publisher to go through their editorial process. But by that time, the manuscript would be in pretty decent shape. But the publisher always set milestones to make sure the writing process was on track; he had already blown the first milestone with the second one right around the corner. Because of Michael's enormous success, the publisher was willing to not make a big deal about the first missed deadline. They extended it. And now that was two weeks away.

Whatever Michael was going through seemed to be

affecting not just our marriage and family life, but his professional life as well.

Maybe he was going through some sort of mental health crisis. The more I thought about that as a possibility, the more it made sense. The sudden change in personality. The drastic mood swings. And what had I done? I'd left him. All alone. What happened if he tried to harm himself? And I hadn't helped him?

I felt sick to my stomach, although that might have been the Long Island Ice Teas. I ran to the bathroom to throw up, but it was a false alarm. I lay in bed as my childhood room spun on me. I was going to be hungover in the morning, but I knew I had to get back to the city as soon as possible. Michael might not have had any issues cutting me and Dash from his life, but maybe it wasn't because he no longer loved us; maybe he was going through something terrible, and during the time he needed me most, I'd left him all alone.

THE NEXT MORNING my head felt like it had a roadwork crew breaking up concrete with the loudest jackhammers known to mankind.

Mom got me the largest coffee cup she had at the back of her cupboards and she filled it to the brim with the black life force. Bless her heart.

"Thank you," I said, almost whispering. Anything louder than that would make the splitting headache I was nursing split even wider, bringing me more pain. This was a cruel reminder of why a couple glasses of wine was my limit nowadays.

Dash must have sensed I wasn't feeling well because he ate his breakfast in relative silence, scrolling on his iPad. *Thank you, Steve Jobs.* When he asked if he could be excused from the table, I was more than happy to say yes. He ran off, leaving me alone with my mother, who gently set down two Advils next to me. I took the pills and washed them down with hot coffee, much to my mother's horror.

"I was just going to get you a glass of water!" she exclaimed.

I shrugged like a petulant teenager. "A cup of brewed coffee is about ninety-eight percent water anyway," I said.

"Really?" She sounded incredulous.

"Yeah, look it up." God, I was being a brat. "Sorry, Mom. I should have stopped after two drinks last night."

"Well, you needed a break from everything you're dealing with."

I couldn't disagree with her logic, though the inside of my head was adamantly disagreeing.

"So what are you planning to do next, dear?"

I sighed. "I can't hide out here forever. Today's the fifth day since I moved out, and I haven't heard from him. I was hoping he'd call right away. But with twelve years of marriage and Dash's wellbeing on the line, I can't play head games. We need to have a serious heart-to-heart, even if he doesn't want to. I can't go on in limbo like this."

At least Dash was on summer break from school, so I didn't have to deal with pulling him out of his classes or anything like that. For that, I was grateful. But I was feeling too queasy and dehydrated to go through that now.

"I'm going to recover today, but tomorrow I'll drive down to the city. Can you watch Dash for me?"

"Of course, honey."

It was set. One way or another, I would soon be getting to the bottom of why Michael had changed so abruptly. Whether he liked it or not, we were going to hash things out between us.

FIVE
MICHAEL

I caught a glimpse of myself in the mirror and couldn't help but cringe — I was a mess. Aside from quick trips to the main house for food, I hadn't left the writing office since Melody had moved out. I'd figured with her and that insufferable attention-needing child gone, I could finally get some work done. But I'd written exactly zero words since they left, which was the same amount I'd managed the previous month when Melody was still here, constantly nagging me about how I'd changed and how I was ignoring her and the boy. Well, no shit; I had to work.

Lydia was on my ass every day. I wanted to block her damned number, but that would just make things worse. I had to get those five chapters written come Hell or high water and keep everyone from riding me before I exploded. That would not be a good thing, but it kept getting harder to hold my true self deep inside.

My phone buzzed. Another mysterious text from *Maybe*.

> You know you can't make that deadline. So make him do it.

How could this mystery person know all this? Another text:

> Make him. What other choice do you have? All this for naught. You're running out of time.

I laid down on the floor and closed my eyes. Strange visions from my head played out like watching a television show on a scrambled signal.

I was right here in my office. Sitting at my desk. But I wasn't staring at a blank page. I was writing. The memory was hazy, almost dreamlike, but I couldn't shake the image from my mind — a faceless man loomed over me, his head encased in a featureless black mask that clung to his face like a second skin. It was smooth and tight, with no visible eyes, mouth, or even the contours of a nose — just an eerie blank surface that reflected the dim light in unsettling ways. The mask made him look inhuman, like some kind of shadow brought to life, and in that moment, as I struggled to comprehend what was happening, I felt a surge of terror unlike anything I'd ever known. Before I could react, before I could even scream, everything went dark, and I was lost to the void.

I opened my eyes and stared up at the ceiling. Had that even happened? My phone buzzed. Another text message:

> It did.

What the hell was going on? I felt like I was losing grip with reality.

I sat up and picked myself from the floor. "You're being pathetic," I said out loud to myself.

I looked at my phone, but the text messages were gone. What the hell? Must be some sort of text eraser app or something.

I couldn't worry about that right now. I knew what needed to be done. I had to accept my limitations and embrace what I'd become instead of pushing it down into the recesses of my memory to pretend that part of me wasn't real.

I didn't do those things. I made a half-hearted attempt to comb my hair with the palm of my hand. It felt greasy and mangled. I stepped outside into the night air. For the first time in months, my head felt clear, knowing what I needed to do. I grabbed the thirty-year-old AlphaSmart tablet from the shelf of the studio and walked back outside to the backyard. Not towards the main house, but out further down the sloping yard, toward the edge of the property. It was time to get those five chapters written once and for all.

SIX
CAPTIVE

I PULLED ON THE LEATHER STRAP AROUND MY neck to ease the chafing. I looked around at what had become my prison. The irony of it didn't escape me. I thought about it every time I looked around the place where I was being held captive.

Refurbishing and remodeling this place had been my passion project, the moment I learned that my new property had one of those underground atomic bomb shelters built in the 50s during the height of the Cold War, as the rich prepared to survive a nuclear bomb attack from the Soviet Union. That feared nuclear attack from the Russians never happened. After decades of paranoia and saber rattling, the Cold War ended in a whimper.

The hatch door on the ground was a heavy steel contraption concealed by a patch of thick, overgrown ivy in my backyard. The previous owners had left it to decay, and the shelter had been abandoned and forgotten for decades. It took a three-man crew and a structural engineer to make the underground shelter safe again.

When I first descended into that shelter, the air was thick with the musty scent of abandonment. Rusted metal beams groaned under the weight of years of neglect, and the concrete walls were stained with dampness, cracked in places where the earth had shifted over time. Faded signs warning of radiation and survival procedures clung to the walls, their edges curling and worn from age. The original furniture — metal bunks, a rickety table, a few battered chairs — stood in disarray, covered in a thick layer of dust. Cans of long-expired rations littered the floor, their labels peeling and unreadable, and a single dim lightbulb flickered weakly from the ceiling, casting eerie shadows across the room.

But where others might have seen decay, I saw potential. I envisioned a sanctuary, a haven that would protect my family. I wasn't worried by the A-bomb, but in the State of California we were waiting for that infamous Big One earthquake. And it was not just threats from Mother Nature or the modern world but from the increasingly invasive demands of life as a bestselling author that concerned me. I had my fair share of creepy fans. So I immediately set to work, pouring time, money, and energy into restoring and transforming the bomb shelter into a modern, first-class underground safe room for us.

The first step was clearing out the old debris, stripping the shelter down to its bare bones. I had the walls reinforced with fresh concrete, sealed up every crack, and waterproofed the entire space to keep out the dampness that had plagued it for so long. The rusted beams were replaced with new, industrial-grade supports, ensuring the shelter's structural integrity for years to come. Once the space was secure, I turned my attention to outfitting it with the latest technology and supplies.

The transformation was remarkable. What had once been a decayed bunker became a state-of-the-art emergency shelter and prepper room. The walls, now smooth and painted a calming shade of gray, were lined with sleek metal shelving units, each meticulously stocked with enough food and water to last over a year. Rows of neatly organized cans, vacuum-sealed packs, and freeze-dried meals stood at the ready, alongside crates of bottled water and medical supplies. In one corner, a high-tech air filtration system hummed quietly, designed to keep the air fresh and breathable no matter what was happening above ground. I didn't skimp on the modern comforts either; a mighty generator could keep the lights on and power essential equipment down here for months. I installed a compact kitchen unit with a propane stove and even set up a small but well-appointed bathroom with a shower.

Despite all the modern upgrades, I kept a sense of the shelter's original purpose alive. I cleaned up and rehung the old warning signs as a nod to the past and even refurbished one of the metal bunks, keeping it in place as a reminder of the shelter's history. It had once been a place of desperation, a last resort against a nuclear threat. Now it was a place of calculated preparedness — my fortress within a fortress, designed to protect me and my family from any danger the world might throw our way.

But I never imagined that I would need protection from my own creation. That the shelter I had so carefully crafted would be turned against me. It was like my own Frankenstein's monster, a paragon of safety that would become my personal nightmare.

I sat on the cot, eating from a can of peaches, when I heard metal grinding above. Someone was opening the hatch door. I set the can aside and stood up. I wasn't about to give this sick bastard the satisfaction of seeing me cower in fear. I was terrified, but I'd be damned if I let him see it. So I waited, standing tall, as he descended into the shelter.

My captor wore the same black, shapeless mask he had on when he'd kidnapped me. In his hands was an old AlphaSmart Neo writing tablet that I kept in my writing studio. I had a habit of collecting relics from the past, things like vintage typewriters and early writing devices I found on eBay. Among them was this 1993 AlphaSmart device —the one he was holding now. What the hell was he planning?

He walked right up to the limit of my chain restraint, stopping just inches from me. He stood there silently, his faceless mask staring back at me.

"Who the hell are you, and what do you want from me?" I demanded, surprised by how steady my voice was despite the bizarre situation I was in.

Without a word, he reached behind his head and began to pull off the mask slowly, like he was peeling off a second skin. The first thing I saw was his pale chin, rough with several days' worth of beard growth. Then, as he continued to remove the mask, it became clear that this wasn't some monstrous thug or twisted creature. He was just a man.

But when the mask finally dropped to the floor at my feet, I recoiled in shock. I had braced myself for anything, but nothing could have prepared me for this. Staring back at me wasn't a stranger or a thug.

It was me.

SEVEN
IRVIN

I grew up poor. I knew how Michael Reed liked to portray his modest origin story of growing up in a working class neighborhood, in a two-bedroom, one-bath rambler home in Fresno. His parents did everything they could so he could have a pleasant childhood despite money always being tight. He spoke of how he had to join the National Guard to pay for college. Well, boo-hoo. That was considered rich where I came from. My family was what's cruelly referred to as trailer-trash hillbillies — but I supposed there was some truth to that.

Just about everyone who grew up in Eastern Kentucky coalfield was just that. It was still considered coal country even though most of the mining companies had closed up shop and left, taking all those jobs with them, well before I was born.

It should be renamed Opiate Country. When I was nine years old, I watched my father die from a heroin overdose. My memories of dear old Pop are him either beating me with a homemade switch or him on the dirty floor of our trailer twitching and foaming at the mouth with a needle dangling from his arm before going still and, just like that, his troubles were over.

Mother was an alcoholic opiate abuser who didn't really have the bandwidth for raising me, so I had to take care of that myself.

My shitty upbringing made me strong, though. I wasn't going to die a junkie in that trailer. School was a road to nowhere, so I dropped out at sixteen.

My economic prospects were limited to the army, welfare, or crime. I didn't like being told what to do, and kowtowing to the government for scraps didn't seem too appealing, so I picked crime. I worked my way from a low-level street thug in Louisville to mid-level criminal kingpin in Cincinnati. I had my lures in several ponds, like identity theft and insurance fraud. But the big money-maker was drugs. It was the most dangerous. The competition was dangerously deadly, and of course you had the state and federal cops on you like white on rice.

The first time someone told me that I looked like Michael Reed was in Louisville. By the time I moved to Cincinnati, Reed's fame went into overload when his bestselling novel, *Whispers in the Dark* was made into a box-office behemoth of a movie starring Tom Cruise, Julia Roberts, and Robert DeNiro. Michael made the rounds on all the morning and late-night talk shows on television. I couldn't even begin to count the times some excited fan shoved a copy of one of Reed's books in my face to sign. Of course I would smile and sign it. I guess that was my first foray into pretending to be Michael Reed. It started harmlessly enough.

My interest in Michael Reed was born from the novelty of being his doppelgänger. Even my name was connected to him. My father was a fan of the Dallas Cowboys, and his favorite player was Michael Irvin, so he named me Irvin Michael Skaggs.

I began reading books for the first time in my life and they were all Michael Reed novels. And was surprised to discover that I loved reading those twisty, mind-fuck type of thrillers he wrote.

If not for being three months older, I could have sworn we were twins. The idea of being a world-famous multi-millionaire author was a pleasant fantasy I would revisit more frequently as my life became more complicated and perilous — common problems of growing up poor and taking to crime, as I had done.

The more I obsessed over him, the more I began to realize that we had a kindred connection. When his book, *The Twin,* was published, I could swear he'd written it with me in mind. I read it three times in a row. From page 1 to 356, and back to page 1.

I began corresponding with him, and though he wasn't responding to me directly, I knew he was getting my emails, and letters. I had one of my hackers in Estonia send me all the private information he could get his digital hands on, and it was a treasure trove of data. It didn't feel evasive, since Michael and I shared a special connection. It wasn't like I was just some nut-job fan. No way. We were family. I figured, since we were one and the same, that I too should write a novel, just like his. But in that aspect, I kept failing. It was so infuriating.

My hacker got me his DNA reports from the DNA4U website, and though the testing report I had commissioned claimed we weren't related, I knew it was wrong. Unable to write like him, I sent him my stories. I believed he would appreciate that and he could turn them into bestselling novels.

It was around this time that I noticed a few flaws in my appearance that kept me from being a carbon copy of Michael Reed. No biggie. Nothing that a plastic surgeon couldn't fix. I had the money, so that wasn't a problem. All it took was eight procedures in two years to fix that. I also stopped taking steroids and working out like a bodybuilder. Michael was a scrawny five-eight. I had bulked up, but it didn't take long to lean out and get my weight down to one eighty, just like Michael. We both had the same dark brown hair and eyes. So that was it. After those minor adjustments, we were one in the same. Mentally, and physically.

I kept reaching out to Michael but not once did he acknowledge me directly, though he did so in many other ways. Like writing and publishing *The Twin* for me. I was overjoyed that he'd dedicated the book to me:

To my twin out there somewhere.

But the more he continued ignoring me, the angrier I got.

I'm not one to be ignored.

Then it happened. Cincinnati police and federal agents came barging into my home. This was expected in my line of work, but still, I didn't see it coming.

I WENT DOWN for drug trafficking, but I had the best lawyer in town, so I was charged on a state level, not federal. Meaning the most I was looking at was ten years, versus forty years federally. I agreed to a sentence of eight years. Lawyer said I would get out in five or six. So, all in all, not a bad deal. It gave me plenty of time to reread all of Michael Reed's novels.

I had two years to go on my sentence when I got a copy of Michael's latest novel, *Intrusion*. It was about a cunning cybercriminal that took over a tech billionaire's life. It was my fucking story. That was when I knew what I had to do. It was what Michael wanted me to do; he wanted me to carry on for him.

In prison I had nothing but time over the next two years to make this come true. It didn't take long for me to realize why he had ignored me for all those year. He was a liar and a fraud. I was the real Michael Reed. That imposter in California was the doppelgänger, not me. And I was going to take back the life that belonged to me.

EIGHT
MICHAEL

I stood there face-to-face with my captor. And it felt like I was looking into a mirror. What the hell was going on? This man, my kidnapper, looked like me — and not like there was just a bit of a resemblance. He. Looked. Like. Me.

Same height. Same eye and hair color. Same body type. And he was wearing my clothes. He could have passed for me.

Oh, God. Then it began to dawn on me. This whole thing was about this — him wanting to be me?

"What the fuck is going on? Who are you?"

He smiled and replied rather cautiously, "I'm Michael Reed."

The way he looked at me made my body tremble. The way he stood there wearing my clothes, looking at me like I was the one that shouldn't be here. It chilled me to the bone. It was a deep yet blank look. What's described by combat veterans as the thousand-yard stare. I didn't even know how to react, and the only words that came out of my slack-jawed face was: "What?"

"I am bestselling author Michael Reed."

"What?" There I went again with my insightful retort.

"I already told you who I am."

"Are you crazy?"

Without hesitation or warning, he stepped up to me and before I could react he punched me in the face. Hard. It was the first time I had ever been punched like that.

I had written about it a lot, but no matter how vividly I thought I was writing about being punched, the reality was far more painful and violent than I'd ever imagined. I now understood what Mike Tyson meant when he said, "Everyone has a plan until they get punched in the mouth."

There was no restraint or pulling back on the punch. It was full force. My head snapped back. A painful, burning sensation spread across my face like a wildfire. Instinctively, I placed both hands on my face to ease the searing pain and to protect myself in case he would do that again. But, luckily, he didn't.

"They tried to tell me in prison that I had schizophrenia. Fucking liars. So don't ever call me crazy."

"Okay, I'm sorry," I said, holding my hands in the air in surrender. I felt so cowardly, but I was chained up down there like an animal by someone who was clearly fucking crazy. I'd just keep that little tidbit to myself.

"What do you want from me?" I asked.

His body demeanor had changed. He seemed a bit more relaxed as he held out the AlphaSmart tablet to me.

"Take it," he snapped when I didn't reach for it right away. So I did as he'd said, hoping to avoid another punch or worse.

"It's fully charged," he said.

"Okay."

"I want you to write five chapters of a new story on it. A new thriller."

"What?"

"You heard me."

"Why?"

"Just do it."

"What if I refuse?"

His face once again hardened. I could have sworn that even his eyes seemed to turn from brown to a deep black, soulless void.

"If you refuse. Well. I'll kill Melody and Dash."

I felt lightheaded as if the blood had drained from my body. My knees wobbled. I knew right then and there that he meant it.

"You have twenty-four hours."

He turned and walked away back to the wall-mounted ladder, and he climbed out of the bunker.

I stood there with the tablet shaking in my hand.

NINE
MICHAEL

I stood there in disbelief for a while. It had been a horrific few months of being chained down here, not knowing what was going to happen to me. But after so long as a captive, left alone, without seeing my captor or anyone else, I'd begun to think that perhaps my captor had died, or maybe he had been arrested, and that eventually someone would find me. I had enough food and water to last me a year. They would look for me, right?

But now, this. Face-to-face with my own goddamned creepy doppelgänger. And he had threatened to kill Melody and Dash, and I knew that it wasn't a bluff. His cold, soulless eyes showed me he was capable of murder. That he had killed before.

I looked at the tablet. It had a long battery life, and limited functionality. It couldn't connect to WiFi or run smartphone apps designed to steal your time away from being productive. This device couldn't even access a printer. It didn't even have a spell check. It was designed to do one thing only: write. It looked like a keyboard with a small screen that wouldn't allow you to see more than four lines of text at a time, each about forty characters long. The text was monochrome — black text on a grayish-green background.

While AlphaSmart no longer existed as a brand, it had developed a cult following from writers who perused the internet looking for second-hand devices to buy that would keep them free of distractions. I bought it to add it to my collection of old writing tools: feather quills, antique writing pens, an MS-DOS computer with the WordStar word processor installed, and about a dozen typewriters. It became one of my unique hobbies once I had money.

Like this shelter, my writing tablet was being used against me to force me to write a novel.

It was as if I had been sucked into the plotline of Stephen King's *Misery*.

What was this psycho's plan? Was he pretending to be me? Had he been living in my fucking house this whole time? Sleeping with Melody. Playing with Dash. Was he working with Lydia? Sure, he looked just like me, but wouldn't they know it wasn't me, for Christ's sake? Had he completely taken over my life? Was he having sex with Melody?

I had to get all that out of my head because no

doubt he would kill them if I didn't give him what he wanted.

Dejected, I sat down, turned on the tablet and started to do what I do best. Write.

For the real-life horror show I was trapped in, being able to write was a welcome relief. I wrote two chapters in an hour. Six thousand words. Damn. Maybe I should have Lydia chain me up and lock me down here on every project from now on.

At first, I thought I would write about a deranged doppelgänger who kidnaps a famous author to take over his life and forces him to write. But that might hit too close to home with that madman. Last thing I wanted was to kick a bear. So I settled on another story. Writing it brought the first modicum of happiness since this nightmare had begun.

As I started the third chapter, I wondered what he was planning to do with this story? I was supposed to be knee-deep on my current project. I had lost track of time, but certainly I had been trapped down here long enough for the first publisher-imposed deadline to have come and gone by now. And my relationship with Lydia was special. She was an agent that rolled up her sleeves with her clients' work. Down in the developmental editing trenches. It was why she was so selective when it came to taking on new clients: She worked hand in hand with them.

Lydia was a savvy, experienced editor, she would

pick up if that nutjob up there was trying to pass his writing for mine. Right?

That had to be why he was now forcing me to write. The pressure was mounting. Lydia could be relentless when it came to work. I smiled at those memories of working with her, laughing, arguing, debating. I missed her. And, God, I missed Melody and Dash. I felt tears welling up in my eyes.

This psycho was going to pass this off as his work, which meant he would hand this to Lydia because I knew she would be hounding him for it. I was certain of it.

She would read this. It was why he'd only given me twenty-four hours. She was waiting for these chapters. That could be my way to signal for help.

I knew the madman would also read it, so I couldn't just type: *Lydia, help me I'm locked in the bomb shelter*. But I might be able to secretly do that without him knowing.

Lydia's sharp editor eyes would pick it up. I was sure of it. I felt my heart beating faster. For the first time since I'd woken up chained down here, I'd caught the faint whiff of hope. A plan to get me out.

I could work in an angle in which perhaps one of the characters used Morse code. But hold on: I didn't know Morse code, so there went that brilliant idea.

Then it came to me. *Écrire en français* — write in French. That was it. I was fluent in French, as was Lydia. I risked that my doppelgänger might speak it too. But what were the odds? I knew that in America almost eighty percent of people spoke English only. I liked those odds and was willing to take the risk.

I wasn't just going to write a paragraph in French asking for help since he could use Google translate if he was clever enough to suspect what I was up to. So I had to hide my message in the manuscript. Embed it somehow. I would break up my cry for help throughout the five chapters. Sprinkle it so the words taken out of context wouldn't raise any red flags with the doppelgänger. But I couldn't make it so hidden that Lydia might read over it and not notice.

I also had to work it into the story so it made sense. I had been at it for hours and I felt exhausted, but I was happy with the results. I came up with a French character who reverted to his native language when flustered or scared.

I read it again. This could work.

The five chapters were complete. Seventeen thousand words in one writing session. A new personal record for me, but not one that I would be celebrating. Amongst all those words, I included three passages in French, and amongst those I hid four words: *Trapped. Bomb. Shelter. 112.*

The 112 was the European equivalent to the US 911 emergency line. I felt a panic attack coming on. Was I being too risky? Putting Melody's and Dash's lives in danger? I had to do something to get out of this hellhole.

I lay down on the cot and quickly fell asleep after an exhausting day of scheming and writing.

I awoke to the sound of the metal hatch door opening. From the hazy light seeping in, it appeared to be morning. Then I heard him coming down the ladder.

I sat up and looked at my captor, and was yet again taken aback at how exactly like me he looked. I could see how he might fool everybody, at least for a while.

"Well?" he said coldly.

I picked up the tablet and held it out to him. "Here you go. Five chapters. Seventeen thousand words. Pretty good, all things considered."

He took the tablet and glared at me. "You wrote seventeen thousand words in twenty-four hours?"

"Nothing else to do down here," I said, trying to be cool about the horrific situation I was in.

"It better not be shit, and you better not try any tricks. Or I kill your family," he said matter-of-factly, as if he were talking about the weather.

Before I could say anything — what could I say to that? — he turned around and headed back above ground, leaving me down here shackled but with a glimmer of hope that my plan would work. *Don't let me down, Lydia.*

TEN

IRVIN

I TRANSFERRED THE DATA FROM THE TABLET TO the computer. I watched as each of the seventeen thousand words danced across the tablet onto the Word document file I had opened. I had been unable to write a single word in months, he'd written this in a day. I felt warm bile bubbling in my stomach. We were one and the same, so why couldn't I do this like he could?

I had tried to write years ago, before I went to prison and during my incarceration, but I couldn't finish anything I started. By coming here and taking my life back from that imposter, I had thought the words would flow. But they hadn't come. I had to rely on him to do what I couldn't do. I slammed both my hands down on the desk.

After I calmed down, I read the manuscript to make sure he wasn't messing with my head. I was expecting something terrible. But it was good. The story was compelling. The prose sang. I wanted to get to know these characters he had created overnight. The foreign words threw me off, but I could see why he'd done that. It made sense for the character to speak in his native tongue. I read it all twice. It was good. I knew Lydia would be thrilled. But I felt betrayed. How could he do this so easily? I hated him.

My phone buzzed. Not again. I feared it was another taunting message from *Maybe,* but it was Lydia. Not sure which was worse.

That bitch was making me furious with her incessant nagging. But now at least I could send this document to get her off my back. It would buy some time to figure out my next move. I sent her a text not wanting to talk to her.

> Emailing 5 chapters over.

She texted back right away:

> Wonderful!! 🙌 😊

She loved to tack on those hideous and annoying emoticons to express her joy. I couldn't stand her. My imposter and his insufferable agent were upsetting me.

But I had the imposter where I wanted. I could use him when needed, like yesterday. But Lydia was out in the wild. As was Melody. How long could I continue fooling Lydia and Melody? They both kept harping on and on about how much I had changed.

Idiots. I should kill them both, but that would send too much scrutiny my way.

As soon as this book was published, I would fire Lydia.

I could divorce Melody, but that would open my life to a cadre of lawyers going through assets and financial records. That could backfire. I had little choice in the matter. Melody would have to die. I could make her body disappear forever, but as the husband, I would be the main suspect. The cops would be on me like I was Scott Peterson and Chris Watts.

Melody's death had to be an accident. And she might as well have the brat with her. I was not about to be a widower and single dad to that brat.

I'd have to table that for now. I emailed the document to Lydia. I felt a sense of relief. But I had a lot of things to figure out.

My phone vibrated. I figured it was Lydia sending more stupid emojis upon receiving the manuscript, but it was *Maybe*.

> The transformation must be complete.

Huh? What does that mean?
Another text message appeared.

> Kill them all.

ELEVEN
LYDIA

SEEING THE EMAIL LAND IN MY INBOX WITH A Word document attached made me so happy. Michael had promised to send me these chapters several times in the past month only to ghost me and then make excuses once I was able to get hold of him. I thought his latest text message was more of the same bullshit, empty promises to buy time and put me off, but I was pleased that he wasn't lying. Finally, the chapters were here.

I downloaded the file, and excitedly clicked on the document to open it. I looked at the outline table on the sidebar of the Word document and, sure enough, there they were: the five elusive chapters.

I looked at the word count: 17,067. *Beautiful.* It seemed Michael might be back on track at last. Most writers struggled with writer's block at one time or another in their career, so this wasn't the first time that getting a manuscript from a client felt like pulling teeth from an non-sedated patient.

But it was the first time I had gone through that with Michael. He had always been my golden child. Not just because my commissions from his books had made me very wealthy but because he was a writing machine. He was prolific. And didn't complain about deadlines, milestones, writing critiques, none of that. He didn't have to wait for the muse to show up. This was his profession, and he took it seriously. An accountant can't tell the boss they can't work because they're not feeling it. Michael was a professional writer who just went to work and delivered an amazing book every single time.

The moment I picked his first manuscript from my slush pile I knew this high school teacher from Modesto was special.

I was halfway through the manuscript when I reached out, knowing that he had probably sent the same manuscript to dozens if not hundreds of other literary agents, and a few of them would see what I had seen, so I had to move quickly. Within three days, he had signed on to be my client. That was more than fifteen years ago. And I was right. I never had to worry about Michael or deal with prima donna bullshit like I had to with other clients. It was why this new hole he had dug for himself seemed so puzzling. Seemingly overnight, a switch had been flipped and Michael could no longer write.

I hoped he still had the goods. I nervously began reading, and to my relief Michael was back. So I got busy reading it.

Michael's story didn't disappoint. And as glad as I was that he had apparently moved past the writer's block, I was still worried about his mental health.

He had written some French passages that did not belong in the story. Stylistically and from a narrative perspective, the choice was fine but didn't seem necessary to move the story forward. Michael was known for his short, straightforward style that would make Ernest Hemingway's work seem bloated and verbose. To him, every word counted as a long as it moved the story forward and the reader was entertained. The French backstory seemed oddly out of place and unnecessary. So I reread it to make sure my mind wasn't playing tricks on me, and that was when I noticed something peculiar.

I'd loved puzzles since I was a kid and one began to emerge from the story.

I reached for my legal pad and jotted down the words in French that seemed odd. Then I drew a line and next to it I wrote down its English counterpart: Piégé | trapped. Bombe | bomb. Abri | shelter. Un | one. Un | one. Deux | two.

Then I wrote it all out in English: Trapped. Bomb.

Shelter. 112. I then crossed out the 112 and wrote 911. So he was trapped in some sort of bomb shelter and wanted me to call 911? It didn't make any sense. Especially with the recent delicate state of his mental health.

Did he want me to call 911? What if I called them? They would think it was a crank call, or if I mentioned the word bomb in the heart of Billionaire's Row, would that trigger a massive law enforcement reaction? This would be the type of story the entertainment tabloids would love. It could turn into a PR nightmare if I were making a mountain out of a molehill.

I had to calm down. Perhaps it was just part of the story that would be explained and resolved later on in the manuscript. All I had were the first five chapters, after all.

Last thing Michael needed was to get on the headlines just because I misconstrued words from a fiction manuscript.

I called Michael, but he didn't pick up, as usual. I remembered that Melody had told me that she and Dash had moved out, so he was all alone in that big house, dealing with his marital problems and the writer's block. And some sort of mental health crisis. What I needed to do was to go see him in person. If this was some sort of cry for help, I needed to be there for him as soon as possible. No more phone calls, emails, and text messages. It takes about eighty minutes to fly from LA to San Francisco and there must be at least twenty flights per day between the two cities, so I called my assistant to book me a flight for tomorrow. Time to get to the bottom of what was going on with Michael.

TWELVE

IRVIN

At noon, the doorbell rang. I wasn't expecting anyone, and I hadn't ordered anything. My fingers hovered above the keyboard, unsure what to do. The sound of the bell echoed through the office again, cutting through the uneasy silence. My heart picked up its pace, a subtle, creeping sense of unease winding through me. I pulled up the doorbell camera feed on my phone and froze.

It was Lydia. *Fuck.*

She was standing right there, on the sidewalk in front of the gate, her expression impatient. I stared at the screen, my pulse quickening. What the hell was she doing here? She hadn't called, hadn't texted — just showed up out of nowhere. I'd sent her the damned chapters she had been hounding me for. So why was she here?

My mind raced, already spinning through the

potential reasons for this visit. None of them were good.

Fuck.

I couldn't move. My mind was stuck in a loop. Lydia knew me too well. She knew something was off, and showing up unannounced could only mean one thing: She had suspicions. She wasn't the type to let things slide, especially when she sensed something wrong.

Did she know about the bunker?

"Come on, Michael, let me in. We need to talk." Her voice crackled through the speaker, a tinge of impatience in her tone.

I didn't respond. I couldn't. I just stood there, staring at the video feed. Lydia wasn't going anywhere, and if I didn't open the door, she'd probably make a scene. The thought of her standing out there, maybe starting to yell or knocking louder, made me feel sick. I could picture the neighbors craning their necks, whispering, making things worse. I couldn't afford to let her stand out there and draw attention to whatever was going on in this house.

My palms began to sweat. The walls felt like they were closing in on me, and I struggled to think straight. She was here for answers, and I wasn't sure what I could tell her that would make her back off. Not after everything that had happened, not after Melody's suspicions. I had worked hard to keep everything together, to keep everyone in the dark. If Lydia got too close, if she saw even the smallest crack in the story I had crafted, it would all fall apart.

My finger hovered over the speaker button. "Lydia, now's not a good time," I said. "Can we talk later?"

A few seconds passed in silence. I watched her on the screen, her brow furrowing, her lips pressing into a thin line.

"Michael, I flew up here from LA because you've been dodging my calls. I'm not leaving until we talk. Now open the freaking door."

Shit.

Her voice had taken on that firm, no-nonsense tone I knew too well. Lydia wasn't bluffing. She wasn't going to just leave. And if she didn't get what she wanted, she would dig. That was the thing about Lydia — once she latched on to something, she wouldn't let it go. She would keep pushing until she got to the truth.

Fuck.

I left the studio and quickly walked across the backyard and into the main house. I glanced around the living room, scanning the space. Everything looked fine, normal. But I felt like the walls were painted with lies, like every piece of furniture had become a part of the deception. Lydia would see through me in a heartbeat. She always had.

"Michael," she said again, knocking harder this time. "If you don't open this door, I'll make a scene."

I winced. That was the last thing I needed — Lydia shouting, demanding answers, drawing the attention of the neighbors. The thought of it made my stomach turn. At least Melody wasn't here because if Lydia and Melody crossed paths... I couldn't even let myself think about that possibility. It would blow everything apart.

I had no choice. I had to open the door, but what could I say? How could I keep her from getting too close? If she saw the tension in my eyes, the exhaustion I'd been carrying, she'd ask questions. And once she started asking questions, there'd be no stopping her.

Taking a deep breath, I hit the speaker button again. "All right, give me a minute."

Lydia sighed audibly, folding her arms and tapping her foot impatiently on the doorstep. I could see the frustration building in her body language, the way her shoulders tensed, the way her eyes darted around like she was expecting answers to fall from the sky.

I turned off the camera feed and walked to the front door, my footsteps heavy with dread. My mind raced as I approached the door, trying to figure out what I was going to say. Every scenario felt like it could backfire. She knew me too well, and there was no way to fake my way through this. I'd have to tread carefully.

With a sigh, I opened the door, and Lydia pushed her way in before I could even greet her. She brushed past me, eyes sharp as they scanned the house like she was looking for something out of place.

"Took you long enough," she muttered, already heading into the living room.

She stood in the middle of the room, arms crossed,

staring at me like she was trying to read my mind. I closed the door slowly, my heart pounding in my chest. I plastered on a smile, trying to ignore the way my pulse was racing.

"Lydia," I said, trying to sound casual. "It's good to see you. I've just been... busy with everything. I sent you the manuscript. You didn't have to fly all the way up here—"

"Cut the crap, Michael," she snapped, her eyes narrowing. "Something's wrong. I know you better than anyone, and I know when you're hiding something. So, are you going to tell me what the hell is going on, or do I need to start digging myself?"

I froze. Her words hit me like a slap in the face, and I could feel my carefully constructed facade cracking. Lydia wasn't here for a friendly check-in. She knew something was off, and she wasn't leaving until she got answers.

I forced a laugh, but it sounded hollow even to me. "It's nothing, really. I've just been stressed with the book, and everything else going on. Melody left me."

"I know. You've been acting weird for weeks. Melody's been calling me, worried sick about you. What is going with you? You're different."

Her words sent a jolt of panic through me. If Lydia was asking these questions, she was already too close to the truth. I couldn't let her dig any deeper, couldn't let her see what was really happening.

"I'm fine, Lydia," I said, trying to sound firm, trying

to convince her with my tone. "Just... tired. It's been a long couple of months."

But Lydia wasn't buying it. She took a step closer, her eyes locked on mine like she could see right through me.

"Michael," she said softly but insistently. "You're not fine. And I'm not leaving until you tell me what's really going on."

Fuck.

THIRTEEN
LYDIA

I ARRIVED AT MICHAEL'S HOUSE UNANNOUNCED, my heart pounding as I pushed the button of the video doorbell on the iron gate. Although Michael's home and writing office sat protected by a tall wall that surrounded the entire property, I knew he was there. Melody had told me he had hardly left the property in months. As I stood on the sidewalk, I noticed the faint glow of the video light from the security camera — clearly, he was watching me stand out there like a fool while a gaggle of tourists meandered by, gawking at the mansions of Billionaire's Row.

I hadn't told him I was coming because I didn't want to give him a chance to make excuses or, worse, disappear while I was flying up here. After almost ten minutes of this silly standoff, the front gate buzzed and clicked open. I stepped inside and closed it behind me, feeling the tension ease slightly as I finally crossed that barrier.

The long pathway stretched out before me, lined with an array of Northern California vegetation — vibrant succulents in various shades of green and purple, their thick, fleshy leaves gleaming under the midday sun. Tall grass swayed gently in the breeze, and clusters of lavender added bursts of color and a subtle fragrance to the air.

I made my way up the stone pathway. I could hear the distant hum of the city beyond the property's walls. The front yard was meticulously landscaped, every plant and stone seemingly placed with the utmost care. Manicured hedges bordered the path, their edges sharp and precise, guiding me closer to the imposing structure of the main house.

The house loomed ahead, its modern design softened by the lush greenery that surrounded it. It was a stunning blend of glass, wood, and stone, designed to complement the natural beauty of the landscape and offering stunning views of the San Francisco Bay. It was all a testament to Michael's success.

When I finally reached the stone steps that led up to the front door, I paused for a moment, taking a deep breath to steady my nerves. I had rehearsed what I wanted to say, but now, standing before Michael's home, the reality of the situation settled in. This wasn't just another professional visit; this was personal, and I was about to cross a line that could change everything.

But if he was going through some sort of mental health crisis he needed my help. Not as an agent, but as a friend.

Michael stood there by the open door. He didn't just look unhappy to see me — he looked tired and disheveled.

"Jesus, Mike, you look like shit," I said. We've worked together for almost twenty years, so I didn't hold back when talking to him. I had to squeeze myself between him and the door frame to make it inside.

He just glared at me. "What do you want?"

This wasn't going well. I stepped inside, uninvited.

"I read the manuscript last night. Several times. It's great so far."

"You could have called or emailed to tell me that. No need to barge in here uninvited."

"I'm worried about you."

"You ain't need to worry about me, that's for damned sure. Was the story no good or what?"

The hair on my arms stood. Michael never talked like that. He prided himself on being well-spoken and eloquent.

"The story was brilliant and well-written as usual."

"So what's the fucking problem?"

"I'm trying to help you. Not as an agent — as a friend."

"Friend my ass. You get your thirty percent cut of what I make."

"I wish. My commission is twelve percent. Did you forget?"

"You know what I mean."

"Look, I don't mean to impose, but you've been off the past three months. There's been a personality switch. And it's not just me noticing it. Melody left you, for Christ's sake."

He turned away from me and headed toward the front door. "I don't have time for this shit."

"What about the odd messages you put into the manuscript?"

That made him stop in his tracks. He turned and looked at me. "What are you talking about?"

"You know, in French?" I quoted back the French lines he had written.

He stood there, puzzled.

I switched to French. "The cryptic messaging you peppered in chapters two, three, and five. It seemed like you needed my help. 911. Remember? So here I am. I want to help you."

He looked at me, lost, like he didn't understand a word of French that I had just said. I switched back to English.

"Michael? Did you understand what I said in French?"

He sighed loudly, then shrugged his shoulders and held his hands out as if to say, *You got me.*

He smirked at me his eyes turned darker.

"You shouldn't have come here, Lydia."

The way he said it made my body start shaking uncontrollably. He was right. I shouldn't have come here alone because I realized this wasn't Michael Reed.

FOURTEEN
MICHAEL

The doppelgänger took away the writing processor and forced me to once again deal with utter boredom of being locked down here like an animal in a zoo.

The living terror I had been dealing with since my captivity had recently been replaced with anger. I had had enough of this. I was going to figure a way to get out of the bunker or I was going to get my hands on that sick bastard. If he killed me, so be it. The supplies I'd stocked down here would last me a year, longer if I rationed. But wouldn't survive that long mentally. And I didn't want to.

Yesterday, when he'd handed me the machine and I was able to write, I had gotten a small piece of my life back. I just hoped Lydia saw my SOS hidden in the words I'd typed. Perhaps the SFPD SWAT units were on their way to rescue me right now.

Writing again had been a wonderful distraction to this nightmare, but it had also served as a cruel reminder of what that asshole up there had taken from me. He had taken away my wife, son, career, my home, my whole damned life lock, stock and barrel.

I was chained up like an abused junkyard dog. I needed to fight back. I had been working on something for the past few days, or had it been weeks? Time was lost down here. My captor had given me enough chain space to get to the food and water supplies. including tin cans of tuna and peaches. I remembered the extensive research I had done a few years ago on prisons for my book, *Pumpkins*. Pumpkin was prison slang for inmates who sport orange correctional apparel while incarcerated. One of the characters was nicknamed Artisan because he was a skilled craft worker who could make objects partly or entirely by hand. Artisan's skill in my story was that he could make prison weapons out of anything he could get his hands on, even from old magazines.

I began working on making a shank. It was slow going since the only tools I had were my hands. But I was able to elongate the cans so they resembled the shape of a knife. I then spent hours sharpening a point on the concrete floor. I hid it in the portable toilet, figuring even this sick psycho wouldn't stick his hand in there. If I could egg him on again to come close to punching me like he had the other day, I might be able to sink this into his jugular vein. It was easier to fantasize doing that than actually doing it, though. I'd never even had a physical fight in my forty-four years on earth. I removed the shank from the toilet and washed it off. I held it in my right hand. Could I do it?

I heard the hatch door opening and my captor coming down the ladder. I hid the shank and waited for the opportunity to use it, praying that I would have enough courage to stab a man in the neck. I wasn't sure I had that in me. I breathed out loudly to calm my nerves.

"You think you're so smart," he said to me.

I shrugged my shoulders, playing dumb. Oh God, he'd found my secret message to Lydia.

I replied with the first thing that popped in my head. "What did I do?"

The imposter got closer, but not close enough for me to shank him. He held out his phone to me and my blood pressure dropped. It was a photograph of Lydia. She was lying on the floor of the foyer of my house. She was face up. The back of her head appeared to be resting on a puddle of blood. Her eyes were partially open. Lifeless. Oh, God.

"Look what you made me do with your stupid little hidden messages. Now she's dead. And that's on you," he said, holding his phone up again with the image of Lydia's dead body.

I just snapped. Any hesitation or doubt I had about being able to kill a human being went right out the window. This thing in front of me was not a human.

"You motherfucker!" I lunged for him, but the chain tightened, yanking me back. I still tried to reach him with both my arms flailing trying to get to him like a bloodthirsty zombie.

The imposter chuckled. It was the first time I had seen emotion from him.

"Finally, you're showing some balls," he said.

Come closer and I'll show you, I thought. But I had to provoke him and get him into the same blind rage as before.

"Some balls you have. You snuck up on me with my back turned. Drugged me. Then you chained me up down here and you stand there where I can't reach you. So, unhook this chain or come closer and I'll show you, asshole."

His face hardened, but he didn't take the bait.

"And you can forget me writing one more fucking word for you," I said.

"Don't make promises she won't be able to keep," he said coldly. That comment took me aback.

"What the hell are you talking about?"

He flipped through what looked to be my phone. And he held it up so I could see it. I looked away. "Fuck you, I'm not looking at what you did to Lydia."

"Oh, don't worry. It's not a picture of that dead bitch. It's a text message from another of your bitches, but this one is alive, for now."

My blood ran cold as I looked up at the phone. It was a text message from Melody that read:

> I'm on my way down to the house.
> We need to talk. I'll be there in two
> hours.

All the anger and fury that had been coursing through my body dissipated in an instant. It was akin to having the wind knocked out of me. Any intention I had of reaching for the shank was gone. My tensed body deflated.

"Don't. Please. I'll do whatever you want. Just don't hurt her."

"Good boy," he said.

I looked down at my feet.

"Those text messages you keep sending me. Hand me that phone, now."

What is he going on about? "What text messages?"

"Ah, come on. You're *Maybe*. Aren't you? I don't know how you did it. I've scoured this place. How did you get a phone to send me those messages?"

"Believe me if I had a phone to send text messages, I wouldn't be sending them to you. The cops would have already broken through the front door."

His face contorted as if he were some sort of machine experiencing a tech glitch.

"I don't have time for this now. We'll get to the bottom of it later. I have to run. I need to freshen up. Melody will be here soon," he said.

"If you hurt her, I'll kill you."

He just laughed and walked away.

FIFTEEN
IRVIN

I WAS BLOWING IT. I GOT OVERCONFIDENT. Everything I had done, everything I had put my body through to take what was rightfully mine, was circling down the drain. It was that damned imposter in the bunker. I was certain he was behind it all. I should have realized he wouldn't give up my life this easily after having stolen it from me for so long. But right now, I had to put Melody at ease for a while longer. Until the time was right to make her disappear.

I went upstairs and showered, letting the hot water scald my skin as I tried to wash away the panic clinging to me. The steam filled the bathroom, clouding the mirror and giving me a momentary reprieve from the reality I faced. I stepped out, wiped a clear spot on the fogged mirror, and stared at my reflection. For a brief second, I didn't recognize the man looking back at me, his eyes wild and desperate, like those of someone teetering on the edge.

I shook off the unease and got dressed, choosing an outfit I knew Michael would wear. I stood in front of the full-body mirror, adjusting the collar of my shirt, and practiced my movements and hand gestures, just as I had done countless times before. "I'm so sorry, honey, for how I've been acting lately," I said, trying to match his tone, his cadence. I cleared my throat, forcing myself to speak and enunciate like him, as I had been doing for ten years. But the words felt foreign, like a costume that didn't quite fit.

A series of text messages buzzed on my phone, one after the other.

> You're not fooling anyone.
>
> Especially Melody.
>
> Can't hide that Kentucky Appalachian twang.
>
> No matter how hard you try.
>
> You're still trailer trash.
>
> No matter how hard you pretend not to be.
>
> You know what you need to do.

"Shut up!" I screamed, throwing the phone across the room. It hit the wall with a dull thud and fell to the floor. My breath came in ragged gasps, my heart hammering in my chest. I had to hold it together. It was the imposter messing with my head. He must have had a phone stashed in the bunker that I'd missed somehow. I had removed the four satellite phones and the ham radio equipment he had down there, but somehow he was able to still send me these messages.

Why wouldn't he contact the police or Melody about what was going on? *Because he's afraid of being found out — afraid they'll realize he's the imposter, not me.* He wanted to steal my life back so no one would find out what he did, and he was playing those games to fuck with my head. Nice try. *This is my life, not yours.*

I took a deep breath and exhaled slowly, trying to regain control. I had meditated in prison and found it did wonders to center me, helping me focus, helping me bend my mind and the nature around me to make things right in the universe. But I hadn't been taking care of myself that way since I got here. Those writing deadlines, the writer's block, that nagging agent — they had all gotten to me. Another deep breath. And slowly I exhaled those worries away.

I walked over and picked up the phone. It wasn't broken, thank God for that. But when I looked at the screen, the text messages from *Maybe* were gone. I stared at the blank screen, my mind racing with confusion, but I couldn't dwell on how he'd made those messages disappear. I had to focus on Melody. I pulled up the tracking app on my phone, the one linked to the device I'd hidden in her car. She'd be here in thirty minutes.

I went back to the mirror, practicing my smile, my expression. "I'm so glad you're back, baby. I'm so sorry for how badly I've treated you and Dash. Please forgive me." I smiled even more broadly, trying to perfect the look of sincerity. Not bad.

I gathered my discarded clothes from the floor and tossed them into the hamper. The bed was already made; I hadn't slept there since Melody left. I hurried downstairs, placing the dirty dishes in the dishwasher and wiping down the counters until they gleamed. Everything had to be perfect.

In the climate-controlled wine cellar, I selected a bottle of Screaming Eagle Cabernet Franc, a $2,000-dollar peace offering. Nothing says "I'm sorry" like a bottle of fine wine that costs more than some people's rent. I carefully placed it on the counter alongside two crystal glasses.

After frantically setting the mood for Melody's arrival, I finally stopped and looked around. The house was immaculate, every detail in place. I checked the app again — she was driving on Pine Street. She'd be here soon.

I took one last deep breath, glancing at my reflection in the window. This had to work. It just had to. But as the minutes ticked by and the anticipation grew, so did the gnawing sense of dread in the pit of my stomach. No amount of preparation could shake the feeling that everything was about to spiral out of control.

SIXTEEN
MELODY

As I drove on our street, I felt anxious. My marriage was on the line. I didn't think anyone, even a Hollywood movie star on their fourth one, took the demise of a marriage lightly. As I pulled into our driveway, my hand trembled. I pressed the button to open the security gate. I steadied myself and drove up to the house.

Michael was waiting for me with a smile. I hadn't seen that in a while. He was dressed nice, and he looked put-together like he used to be, versus the disheveled and bedraggled man I had left behind six days ago. As soon as I walked through the door, he hugged me. I won't lie. It felt wonderful. I've missed feeling wanted. But there was something different in the way he embraced me. I couldn't explain it. How can a tight embrace like this feel so cold and distant?

"I'm so glad you're home," Michael said.

"I'm glad you're finally ready to talk about us," I said, not wanting to let him off the hook just because he'd finally touched me after two months.

"I know, I know, I've been such a fool. How's Dash? I miss him. I miss you both, so much."

The mention of our son's name brought a tear to my eye.

"He misses his father."

"We'll be back to normal, I promise."

I felt a chill because I was not sure if that sounded sincere.

"I have missed you," he said, holding my hand.

I pulled my hand away and looked at him askance because he sure as hell hadn't been acting like he'd missed me or our son.

"Come. Let's talk," he said, leading me to the living room — which was strange; we only used the living room when we had guests. But I followed him there and he had put up quite the show. Lavender-scented candles. Artisanal goat cheese and honey from Marin County. Sourdough crackers. And his prized bottle of wine.

"Screaming Eagle? You said you weren't touching it for at least ten years."

"It's my way to show you how sorry I am."

"You think a $2,000-dollar bottle of wine is going to fix our marriage?"

"No, of course, not. I'm so sorry about the way I've been acting. It's just that damned book was making me crazy. I've never had to deal with writer's block and I got obsessed with it and ignored you and Dash. Treated you both horribly. I guess I just took you for granted, figured you would weather my dark moods, but I didn't communicate with you about what I was going through. I'm sorry."

I sat down on the couch looking across our large living room and looked out the huge floor-to-ceiling window that offered a panoramic view from the Pacific Ocean to the Golden Gate Bridge and into the bay. The fog had burned off, so I could see the multi-million-dollar homes that dotted the steep wooded hillsides of Marin County across the Golden Gate Strait from here into Sausalito down to Tiburon. Angel and Alcatraz Islands stood there like floating sentinels watching me. Magnificent views that even after ten years in this house I did not take for granted, and had missed.

Michael sat beside me and handed me a glass of the expensive wine. I noticed he had brought out the fancy glassware as well. He was pulling all the stops, and it was actually working on me. I was just glad to see that he was now at least trying to work on our marriage.

"Whatever you want me to do, I'll do it. I don't want to lose you forever," Michael said.

I drank the wine, infamously difficult to secure due to its very small production and a snobby and extensive direct-to-consumer waiting list. It was the first time I had tasted the highly coveted Cabernet. It seemed overhyped to me, but maybe it was just because of the confusing flood of emotions I felt just then.

"I want us to see a marriage therapist together," I said.

"Of course. That's a wonderful idea."

I smiled. It was the right answer. After finishing the bottle of wine, we opened a second less expensive bottle and drank that one too. I was feeling warm and tingly and lightheaded. The effects were a combination of happiness that I seemed to be getting my husband back, that he was sorry, and committed to working on our marriage, and of course the two bottles of wine.

And, dammit, I was horny. It had been two months since we had sex. Hell, it had been two months since he'd even touched me. So when he began to gently rub my arm, I was ready to jump his bones. Even if he had told me he hated me and wanted a divorce, I would still probably have had sex if he offered. I giggled out loud at my silly lusty thoughts.

"What's so funny?" he asked with a grin.

"Take me to bed," I cooed.

Thinking of Jerry Seinfeld and George Costanza espousing the wonders of makeup sex on the sitcom made me laugh, but it didn't spoil my mood one iota.

We kissed passionately as we made our way to our bedroom. I playfully shoved him onto our enormous bed. He looked at me, wide-eyed and surprised, almost like it was our first time, and I liked that. I took off his shirt and began kissing his body. I was doing most of the work, but I didn't mind. I helped him take off his pants and began to undress. When I looked down at his lower abdomen in anticipation of what was coming next, the burning desire I was feeling suddenly went out like a backdraft sucking the flames right out of the room. I stopped and sat up straight. I climbed off him and took a closer look because surely my mind was playing a trick on me. I reached out to Michael's abdominal area, near his groin, looking for the ten-inch scar line from the open hernia surgery he'd had two years ago. But his skin was smooth. There was no scar.

I gasped loudly and jumped off the bed, picking up my clothes from the floor. He propped himself up with his elbows, still on his back, and looked at me curiously.

"What's wrong, honey?"

"Your scar," I said. My voice was soft and shaky. My body trembled.

He sat up on the edge of the bed, his face to one side, seemingly confused.

"What scar?"

I took a few steps back as I got dressed.

"What surgery did you have two years ago?" I asked him.

I saw the color drain from his face. Like catching Dash telling me a big lie and calling him out on it.

"What?" he said as he began to get dressed.

"You had surgery two years ago. What was it for?"

He stood up as he finished putting on his shirt but didn't answer.

"Tell me, Michael. What was the surgery you had?"

He looked at me and sighed loudly. His face seemed angry yet relieved. Like he was finally able to come clean about some big secret he had been keeping from me.

He just said, "Fuck."

SEVENTEEN
IRVIN

I COULDN'T BELIEVE HOW DUMB THIS BROAD WAS. All it took was some sweet talk. A few *I love yous*, looking at her with sad puppy eyes and agreeing to marriage counseling — like that was ever going to happen — and she became putty in my hands. I'm sure the two bottles of wine didn't hurt either.

I hadn't planned to sleep with her, I knew that could backfire, but when she started grinding on me and kissing me, and she was a beautiful woman, well, I'm made of flesh and bone like anyone else. I should have gone with my gut, but giving her the cold shoulder hadn't worked. So I would try a different approach.

She was lying on top of me, breathing heavy, her lips and hands all over me, then suddenly she stopped. I was lying back and ready for things to happen when I felt her sitting up. The mood got sucked right out of the room. I looked up at her and she had this look of fright on her face like I had shit the bed or something.

At first, I figured she was having second thoughts about having sex after all our recent problems. And I was fine with that. If she wanted to take things slow, that would buy me time to get everything sorted out on my end. But then she started to ask me about a surgery.

Shit. What surgery?

I knew everything about Michael Reed's life. Information that was public and private. I'd paid a hacker in Estonia a lot of money to get private data on Michael that wasn't available publicly. I couldn't recall seeing anything about a surgery.

This was one of the reasons I had avoided Melody like the plague. She shared an intimate knowledge with the imposter that was too risky for me, so I kept her at arms' length. I just didn't know she would get upset over the way I had treated her to the point that she moved out.

This was a mistake. I gave into my urges, and it backfired.

I was exasperated about all this fucking drama. I wasn't sure how to proceed and the only word that came out of my head as she kept backing away from me with a look of horror was: "Fuck."

Then she began putting on the show. Like I didn't know what had just happened — that she knew the truth. But she regained her composure.

"We're moving too fast here, Michael. You really

hurt me. I'm going back to Modesto, and I'll set up an appointment with a marriage counselor. So, um, I'll call you tomorrow, okay?"

She was lying through her teeth. If I let her leave, she will go straight to the police. She left me no other choice.

"It's fine, sweetheart, I understand. Call me when you get back to Modesto so I don't worry," I said, sweet as pie.

"I will," she said.

She got dressed. I could see her body trembling. As soon as she bent down to put on her shoes, I made my move. I hadn't wanted to do this tonight, but she'd left me no choice. I couldn't let her leave.

EIGHTEEN
MELODY

I WAS TREMBLING, BUT TRYING NOT TO SHOW IT. As I was putting on my shoes to get the hell out of here, the man, who had been pretending to be my husband, jumped on me.

I screamed at the top of my lungs, but I knew it was no use. There were almost a million people packed into the forty-seven square miles that are San Francisco, most of them minding their own business. Besides, this house was built to keep the city noise out, which meant the noises inside the house didn't seep out.

The man was stronger than me, so he easily manhandled me and flipped me over on my back. His brown eyes turned into black spheres that terrified me. I didn't doubt that he was capable and willing to kill me. He might be stronger than me, but I knew one area where I had the upper hand. I just hoped the time I'd spent in self-defense training with light Brazilian jiu-jitsu wouldn't fail me now that I needed to remember it. I figured I would need it out there in the parts of the city where crime was rampant, not in my home. But I made my move.

I wrapped my right arm around his neck and my left arm around his waist. I used my hips to get leverage and make some space between us, and I struck with my knee right into his crotch. He screamed in agony; spittle leaked from his mouth onto my face as he shouted in pain.

"Bitch!"

Before he could recover, I used my legs and back to flip his body off me. I was still facing up, so I kicked my feet and lifted my pelvis, then tightened my upper body to rise to a standing position quickly without using my hands. He was now on the ground moaning. I struck his crotch one more time with the back of my heel, as hard as I could, which made him fold like an accordion as he continued to scream in agony.

"You fucking bitch!"

I ran out of there as fast as I could. I was running so fast that I almost fell down the stairs. He'd recover soon and figure I'd go out the front door, so instead I cut through the kitchen, towards the laundry room where I exited onto the backyard. From there I could make it to a side gate that would drop me out onto Washington Street, where there would be people and cars to help me.

As soon as I flung the door to the laundry room

open, I screamed in horror. Lydia's body was crumpled on the floor like a pile of dirty laundry, a gaping wound in her throat. I'd never seen a dead body before, so my shock and hesitation cost me time. I heard him coming down the stairs and quickly stepped over poor Lydia to make it out to the backyard. It was late and dark, and the fog was so thick it was hard to see, but I just ran. Ran like my life depended on it, because it did.

Even though I couldn't see well through the dark and the fog, and he'd shut off the backyard lights, I knew where the back gate was located, so I beelined toward it.

Suddenly it felt as if the ground under me had vanished, and I plummeted down. It felt like I was suspended in the air for a long time, but in reality I fell hard, and fast, and landed on hard concrete as my entire body radiated with pain. I gasped desperately for air, but there seemed to be none for me. This must be what it felt like to die.

NINETEEN
MICHAEL

Some days I felt my freedom was at hand. I was going to shank my doppelgänger, get the keys to my restraints from the pockets of his dead body, and climb out of this bunker to freedom. Then the self-doubt and fear would take over. *I've never been in a fight. I'm not the most physical type. I'm a writer, not a shanking bad ass.* I was deluding myself by thinking that I could take on a homicidal maniac like the doppelgänger.

I sat on the bunk and pined for my family, feeling sorry for myself, when out of the blue a loud noise made me jump out of my bed. I watched someone come crashing down from above.

At first, I had no idea what had happened or who that was. There was the sound of someone tumbling down and a thud as the body hit the floor. I stood up from the cot in shock as I looked up towards the hatch door and at the person lying on the floor in pain. It was obvious they'd had the wind knocked out of them. It was a ten-foot drop onto concrete floor, so this person could be seriously hurt, even dead if their head had hit the floor. What if that was my captor? If he'd fallen in and died? The body was out of my reach. I would end up chained here with a rotting corpse until my supplies were gone, and I too would die. All these thoughts bounced around my head for a moment, until the person that had fallen turned over in my direction. *Oh, my God.*

"Melody!"

Without even thinking, I ran towards her, but I was yanked back by the chain like an excited dog being pulled by a leash. My body jerked at the pain from the restraint tightening around my neck, but I didn't care. All I cared about was making sure Melody was okay after that nasty fall.

"Melody! Are you alright? Please say something," I pleaded as she rolled on the floor in obvious pain. Her breath was labored.

"Something," she said barely above a whisper, but she seemed to have her sense of humor intact. A moment later, she sat up holding her side. She looked at me and literally shook her head, as if she couldn't believe what she was seeing. She then glanced toward the hatch door.

"Son of a bitch has kept me locked up down here for months," I said, trying not to break down in tears.

Melody slowly got up. She touched her right side and winced.

"You might have cracked a rib," I warned.

She then came straight toward me, hesitant at first as she looked me over suspiciously.

"It's me, babe."

"Michael?" she said, looking up with a befuddled look to her face.

"It's really me."

"How can that be? I just saw you. In our room." Before I could reply, she blurted out, "Let me see your scar from your surgery." She had to catch her breath at every other word because of her injured ribs.

I didn't know what that was all about, but I did as she asked without questioning her. I lifted my shirt and lowered my sweatpants, exposing the surgical scar just as she had asked.

Tears flowed down her face and she rushed towards me and fell into my arms. For a moment I forgot about her injury and squeezed her too tightly, and she squealed in pain.

"Oh, shit, I'm sorry."

"It's okay. Worth it," she said, looking back at me with a smile. "Who the hell is that up there? He's pretending to be you."

Just as I'd feared.

"I don't know, but that psycho up there, he killed Lydia. And he's going to kill us once he finds us here. We need to get the hell out of here right now," I said.

Melody nodded in agreement. She looked up at my restraints and tried to get the neck collar off me, but I stopped her. "It won't budge, I've been trying that since day one. Do you have your phone?"

"No. He attacked me, so I ran away and left my purse at the house. He was chasing me."

"Okay, then you need to go back outside, and go get help."

"I'm not going to leave you down here alone," she said.

"I'll be fine a little while longer; you need to leave right now. Run to the rear entrance door. You remember the code to unlock it?"

"Yes, but—"

"Melody, please, we don't have much time before he comes down here," I said pleading. I didn't care if he killed me; I just didn't want her to get more hurt than she was already or, even worse, for that asshole to kill her.

Then I remembered the toolshed. It had been torturing me this whole time. A metal tool cabinet I had stocked with tools that might come in handy after the Big Quake hit or if the end of the world came. I could see the cabinet standing tall on the other side of the shelter, well out of my reach because of my damn restraints.

"The toolshed!"

Melody ran to it and opened it.

"In one of the drawers I have a fourteen-inch bolt

cutter. It will look like a pruning shear," I said, since Melody was an avid gardener. It worked; right after I said that, she turned around holding up the bolt cutter.

"That's the one!" It felt like my heart was about to explode out of my chest. Melody returned and tried to use the bolt cutter, but I stopped her.

"I'll do that. You need to get out of here before he finds you down here. Go get help."

I could see her hesitate for a moment, but then it must have dawned on her that that was the right move. She handed me the bolt cutter and kissed me hard on the lips. "I love you," she said before turning and running towards the ladder. The probable broken rib had slowed her down, but she must have had enough adrenaline surging through her body to climb up the ladder.

As I watched her disappear above, I frantically began using the bolt cutter. I was nervous, my grip was shaky, and I was weak from being stuck down here, so it wasn't going as well as I had hoped. It didn't help that the bolt cutter was small. It was not designed to cut a chain as thick as the one he'd used to restrain me, but I kept working it, and I could see the metal shavings flaking onto my hands. I just hoped it wasn't too late.

TWENTY

IRVIN

I WAS GOING TO MAKE HER PAY. FIRST FOR KNEEING me, and then for kicking me in the balls. The pain was still searing, a white-hot agony radiating from my groin, but the rage that surged through me was even more intense. No one made me look like a fool. I didn't care anymore what had happened here. My plan, years in the making, was falling apart around me. All I knew for sure was that Melody would die today. That was a certainty.

I struggled to get to my feet, each movement a reminder of the blow she had dealt me. The sound of her footsteps echoed in my ears as she flew down the stairs. I pushed the pain deep down, picked myself up, and gave chase. But she had a good head start, and she'd been living here for ten years — she knew every nook and cranny of this place better than I did.

I fumbled for my phone, pulling up the video security app to see where she'd gone. I watched the front door feed, but there was nothing. Frustration gnawed at me as I switched to the backyard camera, rewinding the footage for five minutes. And then I saw her — like a ghost materializing out of the dark and fog — running toward the back wall of the property.

There was a rear entrance there, I remembered, one that allowed for a discreet exit onto Jackson Street instead of out the front door onto Washington Street. A surge of panic washed over me; if she reached that back door and got out, she'd find help quickly. Everything I'd worked hard for here would unravel. I felt dejected, my legs trembling with pain and anger. She must have already made it outside. Why couldn't I hear the approaching sirens?

But then, something unexpected happened. I watched the screen, my breath catching as I saw her drop suddenly, disappearing from view. What the hell? That was where the underground bomb shelter was located. In my haste to exit the bunker earlier, I must have forgotten to close the hatch door all the way.

I rewound the footage and played it again, watching her stumble and fall inside. I stared, waiting for her to reappear, to climb out and continue her escape, but she didn't. She must be stuck down there. That was a long drop. She might have cracked her skull or broken her neck during that fall. Those thoughts sent a thrill of dark satisfaction through me that made me smile.

Without another second's hesitation, I bolted out of the house, running across the backyard like a man possessed. My heart pounded, not just from the exertion but from the adrenaline coursing through my veins. I was only a few feet away when I saw her pop out of the hole like the vermin she was. I couldn't have asked for a clearer divine sign — this was my life I was fighting for, not that fucking imposter's down in that hole and his whore wife's. Tonight it ended.

With the agent out of my way, these two were next. Once I killed them, then I could reset my life and start over. Ship that brat off to a boarding school in Timbuktu as soon as possible. But I had to focus; I was getting ahead of myself.

As soon as she made her way outside, I noticed she was struggling, clutching her side. She must have gotten hurt when she fell. She moved slowly, painfully shuffling toward the rear entrance. It was almost comical, watching her pathetic attempt to escape. She had grit, I had to give her that much. But she was weak now, broken.

I jogged down toward her, and before she could turn to face me, I struck. My fist slammed into her ribs, right where she had been holding her side. The scream that tore from her throat was too loud, dangerously loud. We were outside now, after all. I couldn't afford to have anyone hearing this. Before she could scream again, I scooped her up like a ragdoll, her body limp and helpless in my grip, and dragged her back to the open hatch. With one brutal motion, I tossed her down into the hole.

I leaned over the opening for a moment, catching my breath, watching her as she fell back inside. But she managed to grab one of the rungs of the ladder, breaking her fall slightly. It was still painful from the sound of the scream that echoed up the tunnel as she hit the side of the wall then dropped on the floor with a heavy thud. I watched her lying there, motionless.

TWENTY-ONE
MICHAEL

I HAD BEEN TRYING TO CUT THE CHAIN WITH THE bolt cutters when I heard Melody screaming from above. The bastard had gotten to her. I worked more frantically at the chain, but then I saw her fall back down again. She was able to slow her fall this time, but she still landed awkwardly and hard. She lay there motionless. Oh, no! I imagined the worst. She was dead.

"Melody, are you okay?"

After a few seconds, she recovered and sat up slowly. "I'm sorry, he caught up to me," she gasped, tears streaming down her face.

My heart twisted at the sight of her — my Melody, broken and terrified. "It's okay, babe, we're going to be okay," I said, trying to inject some confidence into my voice. But the words felt hollow, even to me. I didn't believe them, and by the look in her eyes, she didn't either.

I watched as she tried to pull herself up, her face contorted in pain. That son of a bitch — he would pay for this. But deep down, I knew that our chances of getting out of this alive were slipping away. I went back to cutting the chain that bound me, but the metal was too thick and my hands shook with fear and exhaustion.

I then heard him coming down the ladder. Melody made her way towards me. The doppelganger stood there, surveying the scene. He looked over at the toolshed with its doors open then turned his glare full of hatred towards us. I tried to hide the bolt cutter behind my back, but he saw it. He pulled out a pistol from the back of his waist and pointed it at me and Melody. Both of us cowered from looking up the barrel of a gun.

"Slide that bolt cutter towards me," the doppelganger said.

"All right, all right," I said, tossing it in his direction. It clunked off the concrete floor before landing at his feet.

Melody was doubled over in pain, but she did a double take between me and the evil doppelgänger. "What the hell is going on?" she said.

"I don't know. I woke up here chained up and this motherfucker that looks just like me has held me captive ever since. Forcing me to write."

"Liar!"

Melody and I both flinched at the ear-piercing screech from the doppelgänger. I hadn't expected that reaction. He double-timed towards us with his arm raised, waving the gun in our faces.

"I'm Michael Reed. You're the imposter. Not me!"

I looked at Melody, not knowing what to do or say; from the frightened look on her face, she was thinking the same thing: *This guy is crazy, and he's going kill us both.*

TWENTY-TWO
MICHAEL

My doppelgänger stood before Melody and me as we clung to each other, our arms intertwined. When he'd worn the faceless black mask, he'd never spoken. Since he'd taken off the mask, he'd treated me aloofly and was usually calm. He spoke in a matter-of-fact manner even while threatening me. I had rattled him the one time, when he punched me. But now he seemed even more unhinged, like he was falling apart from having to deal with the reality that he wasn't me.

It seemed telling him he wasn't the real Michael Reed was the surefire way of making him lose his mind even further. Not a button I wanted to keep pushing as he pointed a gun in my face. But it was a way to get him close enough for me to shank him. I kept staring at the gun as he went off on me.

"You stole my words, my life, you think I was going to let you get away with that forever?" he said.

"It's yours. Take it. Just let us go," I pleaded.

"It's not yours to give away what doesn't belong to you. It belongs to me," he seethed.

"But you need my help to write the books. Just like I did for the first five chapters. I can help you finish that book," I said, desperate to buy Melody and me more time.

The doppelgänger ignored me as he pointed the gun at Melody and barked out orders, "Come on, let's go, bitch!"

"Where are you taking me?" Melody asked.

"Don't worry about it. Get your ass above ground," he said, grabbing Melody by the arm as he shoved her towards the ladder. She flinched in pain from her injuries.

"If you hurt her, you'll have to write your own fucking book. I don't care if you kill me. You understand?"

The doppelgänger turned and glared at me, but he didn't say anything as he continued shoving Melody towards the ladder.

"Up you go," he said to her as he pressed the barrel of the gun to her back.

Melody did as she was told. I kept tugging at the chain. Pulling and yanking as I yelled at the doppelgänger.

"You let go, you sick son of a bitch!"

He continued to ignore me.

I had to strike that nerve once again. "I'm the real

Michael Reed, not you. Don't you forget it, asshole. You can't write a fucking word without me because you're a fraud. An imposter."

It worked. That stopped him cold, as he blew another gasket. He turned and ran at me. "It was you sending me those text messages!"

I didn't know what he was talking about. I had no phone, no way of sending him text messages, but I wanted him to leave Melody alone so she could escape, and it was working, so I went ahead and took credit for them.

"That's right, asshole. It was me. I sent you those text messages. Me. The real Michael Reed."

My doppelgänger was now ranting and raving; I didn't even understand what he was saying. He was like a street preacher speaking in tongues. But such was his blind rage that he didn't realize that I had worked on the chain enough with the bolt cutter and had been secretly tugging at it the whole time. As soon as he came within an arm's length, I yanked on the chain one final time as hard as I could and heard the chain links clunking onto the concrete floor. The doppelgänger heard that too, and he looked down as I lunged at him with the shank.

But he saw it coming and side-stepped as the shank grazed his chin instead of sinking into his neck. He regained his footing while at the same time grabbing my arm and twisting so hard I thought he was going to rip it out of its socket. The shank I had spent so much time on, slowly sharpening it, flew out of my hand and joined the pieces of metal from the chain on the floor as it skittered away from my grasp. *Dammit!* I'd failed.

I looked up as the doppelgänger kicked me in the chest, which made me fall back. My counterattack had failed. The doppelgänger had raised the handgun and aimed it at me when Melody came up behind him and stabbed him with the shank that she had picked off the floor.

The doppelgänger turned to face her, pointing the gun at Melody, and he pulled the trigger. I watched my worst nightmare come true as Melody fell backward, a crimson flower spreading ominously across her chest.

As far as I was concerned, my world ended that night, down in that fucking bunker. All of this had happened because some deranged lunatic wanted my life.

I don't remember much after Melody was shot. Everything turned to black. I just wanted to kill my doppelgänger. I remembered bum-rushing him and falling hard on top of him as the gun skittered away. And I just began pummeling him.

I didn't know I had that sort of rage and hatred inside of me. It felt as if my soul had left my body and I watched my physical being attack the doppelgänger from above, as if I were just a spectator. I had written about my characters having out-of-body experiences before, but I had never had one until that night. I was going to kill him. And I relished embracing the darkness as my world turned black.

TWENTY-THREE
MELODY

My recovery was agonizingly slow. I was a wreck — a shadow of myself. Three broken ribs, a grade-four concussion, and a gunshot wound to the chest.

And the hits had kept on coming as I slipped into septic shock, a life-threatening condition triggered by a blood infection that my body struggled to fight off. My immune system, which should have been my protector, turned against me.

I don't remember any of this. The memories of that time are a blur, erased by the pain drugs and the haze of a medically induced coma. I would later learn that I was strapped to a ventilator, fighting to survive without even knowing it. My mother would tell me that the doctor advised her to say her final goodbyes, to prepare my end-of-life arrangements. The doctors told her my chances of survival were slim.

But somewhere, in the deep recesses of my mind, I was aware of what was happening to me. Not of the hospital room, or the machines beeping and whirring around me, but of something else — something dark, something terrifying. The only memories I have from that time are fragmented, disjointed, like pieces of a puzzle that never quite fit together. I'm not sure if they are memories or dreams — nightmares, more like it.

In these visions, I kept seeing Michael. He was standing there, just a few feet away from me, smiling that wide, familiar smile that I had loved for so many years. But something was wrong. He was surrounded by blackness, like he was in a void —an endless, suffocating blackness that seemed to swallow him whole. I wanted to reach out to him, to pull him back, but I couldn't move. My body was paralyzed, trapped in this strange limbo. I tried to call out to him, to ask him where we were, but no sound came out. My throat was tight, my voice strangled.

And then I saw him — his doppelgänger. He was creeping up behind Michael, moving slowly, deliberately, as if he had all the time in the world. The air around him seemed to shimmer with a dark energy, something malevolent and wrong. Evil. My heart raced with fear, pounding in my chest like a drumbeat. I tried to scream, to warn Michael that the doppelgänger was right behind him, but my voice was lost in the void.

"Turn around!" I was finally able to yell, but he couldn't hear me. He just stood there, smiling at me, his arms outstretched, ready to embrace me and take me into the void.

As the doppelgänger drew closer, his face came into focus. It was the same as Michael's, but different — twisted somehow. His smile was too wide, his eyes pitch-black. He was right behind Michael now, so close that he could reach out and touch him. And then, slowly, he did. He placed his hand on Michael's shoulder, and Michael didn't flinch. He didn't move at all. He just kept smiling at me, oblivious to the danger right behind him.

The doppelgänger's gaze shifted from Michael to me, and his smile widened even further. He leaned in, his lips close to Michael's ear, but his dark eyes never left mine. "I'm the real Michael," he whispered, his voice dripping with malice.

The words sent a shockwave through me, a cold, paralyzing fear that gripped my heart and squeezed it. I gasped for air, my chest tightening as if a vise was closing around it. The darkness around me seemed to pulse, growing thicker, more oppressive, until it was all I could see, all I could feel. I was drowning in it, suffocating under its weight.

And then, just as suddenly, there was light — blinding, searing light that cut through the darkness like a knife. The light was so bright it hurt my eyes, piercing my skull with a sharp, stabbing pain. I tried to shield my face, but my arms wouldn't move. I couldn't escape it. The light grew brighter, hotter, it seared my face until it was all-consuming, it burned away the darkness.

I felt a rush of air that was cool and sharp; it filled my lungs and pulled me back from the brink of the void. The light wasn't just light from the hospital room — it was life, it was breath, it was the world calling me back from the edge. I felt hands on me, pulling me, guiding me, voices of medical staff speaking over me. I couldn't quite understand what they were saying. But it felt as if they were dragging me out of that black void, out of the nightmare, back to the land of the living.

The brightness dimmed, softening into the fluorescent glow of hospital lights. The harsh beep of monitors filled the air, grounding me in reality. I blinked, my vision clearing, and for the first time in what felt like an eternity, I could see. I could breathe.

The faces of doctors and nurses hovered above me, their expressions a mix of relief and exhaustion. My body ached, every inch of me screamed in pain, but I was here. I was alive.

I faded out again, waking up in a hospital room. My mother's face appeared next, her eyes red and swollen from crying. Her hands trembled as she touched my face. She spoke to me, her voice choked with emotion, but I couldn't focus on the words. All I could think about was the nightmare — the vision of Michael and his doppelgänger, the darkness, the fear.

Had it been real? Or was it just a figment of my fevered imagination, a hallucination brought on by the infection and the drugs? Or was it something more — a warning, a glimpse into a reality that I wasn't supposed to see?

I didn't have the answers, but one thing was clear: I had been given a second chance. I had been pulled back from the edge, dragged out of the darkness by some force I couldn't comprehend. But the darkness was still there, lurking at the edges of my consciousness, as if waiting for the right moment to strike.

I thought about my son. My poor child must be worried sick. The first word out of my mouth: "Dash?"

My mother smiled. "He's fine, honey. He'll be here soon."

That news filled me with a peaceful calm I hadn't felt in a long time, but it was short lived, as I didn't even know where I was. I asked my mom.

"You're at the UCSF hospital in Parnassus," she told me.

"Is Michael okay?"

My mom smiled and she looked up at the door and nodded at someone standing there. "The doctors recommended we do this slowly after what you both went through," my mom said. A man walked in with the aid of a cane and came rushing to my bedside. It was Michael. But seeing him made me flinch. My body stiffened. The blood pressure machine began to beep faster. "It's okay honey," my mom said, trying to reassure me.

I looked at the man standing by my bed. He was

battered and bruised. He looked like Michael. But so did that other son of a bitch who had tried to kill us both. How could I have been fooled that way? To not recognize my own husband. What was wrong with me?

"It's really me, babe," he said. I wasn't sure what to believe. I felt a panic attack coming on. Then I heard the calming voice of another man saying, "We can try this later. She needs time after what she's been through." And the man claiming to be Michael nodded and turned back to me. "I'll be right outside in the waiting room. Whenever you're ready."

Ready for what? To carry on with my life like before? I didn't think that was possible, and it made me start sobbing.

TWENTY-FOUR
MELODY

THE NEXT FEW WEEKS WERE A WHIRLWIND. EAGER to leave the hospital, I clung to the hope that I could go home soon, provided my test results stayed steady and the infection remained under control. I was so pumped up with antibiotics that I felt nauseous and had hardly eaten anything these past few weeks. I was weak and light-headed.

The only true, unadulterated joy in my life during that time was being reunited with Dash.

The man with the gentle voice who had asked my family to give me more time turned out to be Dr. Evan Kanzaria, a psychiatrist. At first, I was offended. Why had a psychiatrist been assigned to my case? I wasn't the crazy person that had attacked us. But I calmed myself. I was surprised that the stigma of mental health was still so entrenched within me. My body had gone through a lot of trauma, and not all physical.

Dr. Kanzaria didn't push me. "Whenever you're ready to talk, I'm here for you," was all he said as he ducked out of a busy room that seemed to be Grand Central with doctors, nurses, and technicians coming and going around the clock. Did they really need to wake me up at two in the morning to check my vitals? Apparently they did. I was ready to go home.

I ALSO MET with Inspectors Dale Ganns and Heather Sanchez with the San Francisco Police Department, who were handling the investigation. Although they shared frustratingly little about their investigation because it was "ongoing," I did learn more about the F5 level tornado that had swept through our lives, tearing it apart.

Its name was Irvin Michael Skaggs. A man who apparently resembled Michael so much that he had become an obsessed fan, undergoing several plastic surgery procedures until eventually he had become delusional, believing that he was actually Michael Reed and that Michael was an imposter who had stolen his life. Thinking about it made my head spin.

"He was diagnosed with schizophrenia. But since getting out of prison he stopped taking his meds so the shrinks think he was experiencing psychosis, disorientation and hallucination when he targeted you and your husband."

Ganns had an unsettling calmness, his lean frame and bald head giving him a severe look that matched his piercing, almost black eyes. Beside him stood Sanchez, fierce and compact, her intensity softened only by her dark, wavy hair. Together, they were a well-oiled machine — Ganns the quiet storm, Sanchez the lightning strike.

Ganns reached out to shake my hand, and I noticed how large and strong his hands were.

"Mrs. Reed," he said, his voice low and steady, carrying just a hint of gravel.

Inspector Sanchez stood beside him, her eyes locked on mine. There was a fierceness in her gaze, a silent challenge that made me want to straighten my posture. "We're here to talk about what happened," she said, her voice firm but not unkind. There was an undercurrent of empathy there, but it was clear she wouldn't let it get in the way of finding the truth.

I couldn't help but feel a little on edge around them. Something about Ganns and Sanchez made it clear they were people who got answers, whether you were ready to give them or not. They radiated a kind of quiet menace, the kind that made you feel like you were under a microscope, being dissected piece by piece. But a strange comfort lay in knowing that they were the ones handling the investigation. If anyone could get to the bottom of this mess, it was them.

"We just wanted to go over the timeline of everything that went down," Ganns said.

"Again?"

"Yes, sorry; I know it's frustrating to go over and over this, but it's the only way to make sure we know what happened."

I rattled off what had happened, yet again. "I told you, this Skaggs person kidnapped my husband, impersonated him. When I figured out he was an imposter, he tried to kill me, and Michael. He had already killed Lydia, so I knew what he was capable of. But we got the upper hand, and Michael killed him." Ganns and Sanchez both scribbled into legal pads. "In self-defense, of course," I added quickly.

"And you didn't realize Irvin Skaggs wasn't your husband for fifty-eight days?" Sanchez asked.

I swallowed hard, the weight of that realization settling in. Fifty-eight days. I felt like such a fool.

"It wasn't until you noticed he was missing the surgical scar from your husband's hernia surgery?" Ganns added.

They asked me this matter-of-factly, without judgment, but I couldn't help but feel judged and defensive about it. I felt stupid.

"I know it sounds crazy, but that man was a carbon copy. You told me he had plastic surgery to look even more like Michael. So yeah, he fooled me. But his whole personality changed and he could no longer write. That he couldn't mimic," I said, feeling like I had to explain myself for not knowing sooner.

I cleared my throat and added, "I guess I'm lucky

that we kept his hernia surgery secret, out of the public eye, so that the imposter didn't know about it."

"Sick bastard would have probably given himself that scar had he known," Sanchez said.

"Probably," Ganns added, making me feel slightly better over this crazy, messed up situation.

It was bad enough that a media frenzy about our case was in full force. The headlines were nauseating: *Real Life Misery,* and my personal favorite, *Famous Author's Wife Had No Clue She Was Sleeping with Look-Alike Killer.* And non-stop references to the movies *Dead Ringers* and *Us.* To them it was a fun twist to an already screwed-up crime, with a famous author to make it even more titillating for mass consumption for the general public. Except it was my real life. It wasn't fodder for true crime entertainment news outlets and podcasts.

My mom and Michael begged me to stay away from social media, but I couldn't help it, and I saw the nasty comments about how stupid I was and how I was probably in on it to kill Michael with my lover so I could inherit his vast wealth. I had married Michael when he had nothing, and now social media randoms accused me of being a gold digger. It was a nightmare on top of another nightmare.

"What about those text messages? He ranted on and on about them, accusing me and Michael of sending him?"

"Our forensic techs have scoured all phones and

cloud accounts and there weren't any text messages sent that match those he claimed he had received under the alias of *Maybe*. Even if he had deleted them, we would have recovered them. So they don't exist," Ganns said.

"It was all in his head?" I asked, mostly wondering out loud.

Ganns shrugged. "Aside from the schizophrenia, Irvin Skaggs had a known habit of overindulging in hallucinogenic drugs like LSD, mescaline and mushrooms. Some people that abuse hallucinogenic drugs can re-experience the effects of the drug days, weeks, or even years after they used it."

"The shrink called it hallucinogen persisting perception disorder — HPPD," Sanchez added.

My body trembled as I thought about how I'd lived with this demented man for months. How I let him near Dash. My eyes always teared up when I considered the danger I had unwittingly exposed my son to.

I was glad when they changed the subject. The detectives asked a few more questions about our daily routines, and after they'd forced me to relive the worst part of my life again for about forty minutes, Ganns and Sanchez seemed satisfied as they put their stuff away, getting ready to leave.

"So what happens now?" I asked them.

"Well, as complicated and strange your case is, it all does boil down to a simple case of an obsessed stalker turning into a violent kidnapper and murderer.

We still need to ask more questions of your husband, but he's struggling with all this, so we're giving him space," Ganns said.

"Don't worry. We'll be out of your hair soon," Sanchez said with a smile.

"No offense, but I hope so," I said.

"None taken," Ganns said as he tapped the edge of my hospital bed before he turned around and left with Sanchez on his heels.

I sat there for a moment alone, taking it all in. My mom had moved into our house to help take care of Dash since Michael was also in recovery. Taylor and Jessica, bless their hearts, had been coming down from Modesto to help out and give my sixty-nine-year-old mother a break. And although I was ashamed to admit it, I was hesitant to leave Dash alone with Michael.

Just then, as if to worsen my guilt, Michael walked into my room. And I couldn't help but visibly tense up whenever he would enter. I could tell my visceral reaction at seeing him hurt him, but part of me wondered: Was that really my husband standing in front of me?

TWENTY-FIVE
MELODY

I WAS FINALLY BEING DISCHARGED FROM THE hospital the following day. I sat in a chair, staring out the window at UCSF Parnassus, the sterile scent of antiseptic clinging to the air. The chair wasn't comfortable, but it was a small comfort to be out of the bed, to feel a little more human after everything that had happened.

The window offered a breathtaking view of the city that almost made me forget I was in a hospital. I could see the top of the towers of the Golden Gate Bridge piercing through the fog in the distance while the Marin Headlands loomed behind it. The bay sparkled under the late afternoon sun, a deep blue that matched the sky.

The view should have been uplifting, but instead felt surreal — like staring at a postcard. Even in the confines of a hospital room, with its white walls and beeping monitors, San Francisco offered a glimpse of its splendor. The city was alive, vibrant, pulsing with an energy that seemed to mock the stillness of my current existence. It was almost cruel, how beautiful everything looked from up here while I felt so trapped, so broken.

Yet I found solace in the view. It reminded me that there was a world beyond these walls, a world that still held beauty and promise, even if it felt distant from where I sat. The city was a reminder that life went on, that there was something to hold on to, even in the darkest of times. The city out there, so beautiful and iconic, had survived earthquakes, fires, and countless other challenges.

And as I sat watching the fog wrap around the bridge and the hills, I told myself that I could survive this too. That somehow I would find my way through the darkness and come out on the other side, just like San Francisco always did.

My thoughts dissipated as I heard a soft knock and turned toward the door. My body stiffened. Michael stood there, his expression filled with concern.

"Looked like you were in some deep thoughts," he said, his voice gentle.

I forced a thin smile, though it felt like an effort to do just that. Dash was the only person who could truly brighten my day right now.

"Are you excited to go home?" he asked, a hopeful tone creeping into his words.

I hesitated, guilt washing over me. The truth was, I was terrified. The thought of going back to that house filled me with dread, but I couldn't bring myself to admit to that. Michael must have sensed my unease because he said, "Maybe we should sell the house. Too many terrible memories there now. We can find a new home to rebuild our lives. Maybe down in Southern California. Get out of this damned fog and chilly summers."

His suggestion caught me off guard. Michael loved living in San Francisco. It had been his idea to move here from Modesto, and he had always been disdainful of Southern California. He would say that LA was plastic and phony, full of people more concerned with appearance than substance. San Francisco, with its quirky, laidback, eclectic hippie vibe, had always been more his speed.

The thought of him wanting to leave now, after everything that had happened, seemed odd. But maybe a change of scenery would help us heal, give us a fresh start. And that property was now a den full of bad memories. Why not start over somewhere else? I didn't want to have that conversation right now.

"We can figure that stuff out later," I said, trying to keep my voice steady.

"Sure, of course," he replied, but there was a hint of frustration in his tone.

He moved to one of the visitor chairs across from me and sank into it, a forlorn look on his face. I could see the weight of everything we'd been through etched in the lines around his eyes, but I didn't want to admit that I was scared of going home with him. My mom was planning to go back to Modesto in a few days. Maybe Dash and I should go with her, just for a while. But I knew I couldn't go on like this, living in fear, doubting the man in front of me. It was eating me alive.

I hated myself for it, but I needed to know.

"Michael," I said softly, my voice trembling slightly. He looked up at me, a flicker of hope in his eyes as if he were almost excited that I had said his name.

"Don't get mad at me," I continued, watching as his expression shifted to one of worry.

"Um, sure, I guess. What is it?" he asked tentatively.

"I need to see it."

He frowned, confusion knitting his brow. "See what?"

"The scar from your surgery."

For a moment, time seemed to stop. His entire demeanor changed, and I could see the shift in his posture. His shoulders slumped, and his eyes hardened as he stared at me. I inconspicuously moved my thumb to the nurse call button, ready to press it if I needed to.

"Are you serious?" he asked, his tone dripping with anger.

"I asked you not to get mad," I whispered.

He let out a long sigh, his frustration now evident.

"I know, but come on, Melody. You think I'm that sick fuck?"

"No, of course not. Well. I don't know... I'm just confused and scared. I'm sorry," I said as tears began to trickle down my face.

Seeing my tears seemed to soften him. His face relaxed, and he watched me for a moment, as if trying to decide whether to be angry or understanding.

"Hey, now. Okay, okay. I get it," he finally said, standing up. He pulled his shirt out of his jeans and lifted it, positioning himself so I could see his abdominal area. And there it was — the scar.

My heart pounded, the thudding sound loud in my ears as I stared at it. It looked like the scar from his surgery, the one I had seen so many times before. But something still didn't feel right. I leaned closer, but he put his shirt down.

"Did that help?" he asked with both exasperation and concern.

I nodded, though I wasn't sure if I was convincing either of us. The scar was there, but the doubts still lingered in the back of my mind, gnawing at me. The man in front of me looked like Michael, acted like Michael, but I couldn't shake the feeling that something was off. It was like a puzzle where all the pieces seemed to fit, but the picture still looked wrong. I had been fooled for almost three months before.

"Thank you," I finally managed to say, my voice shaky.

"We'll get through this, Melody," he said, softening. "We'll rebuild our lives, I promise."

I wanted to believe him, I really did. But as I sat there, staring into his eyes, I couldn't help but wonder if the man making that promise was really my husband.

TWENTY-SIX
MELODY

Hospital policy required an orderly to wheel me out, which was fine by me. My body ached, and the painkillers had left me lightheaded, so I wasn't about to argue.

As desperate as I was to leave the hospital, I couldn't help but feel dread at going back to that house, the place where everything had fallen apart, where my life had been ripped to shreds by Irvin Skaggs.

Michael and I sat in the backseat of the black SUV, driving through the streets of San Francisco in silence. The closer we got to the house, the more I felt that dread turning into something darker, something more sinister.

Michael's hand rested on my knee — a gesture meant to comfort me, but all it did was set my nerves on edge. His touch felt foreign, like a stranger's, and I had to resist the urge to pull away from his hand.

I kept my eyes fixed on the window, watching as the familiar sights of the city passed by in a blur. The tall buildings, the cable cars, the busy streets — everything looked the same as it always had, but it didn't feel the same. I supposed that would be the new normal for a while.

"We'll be home soon," Michael said, his voice calm. I couldn't bring myself to respond; the word "home" felt like a lie.

Once our dream home, the Pacific Heights mansion now felt like a prison, a place where nightmares had taken root. The memories of what had happened there — of the doppelgänger, of the terror I had endured — clung to me like a dark cloud, suffocating me.

I forced myself to nod and smile, but I couldn't look at him. I couldn't shake the feeling that something was wrong, that the man sitting beside me wasn't really Michael. I had seen the scar, but even that hadn't erased the doubts in my mind. There was a coldness in his eyes, a hardness that I didn't recognize, and it terrified me.

The SUV turned onto our street, and my heart began to race. I could see the house in the distance, its grand facade hovering over us like a dark sentinel. It looked the same as it always had, but it felt different now — ominous, foreboding. The memories of that night flooded back, and I had to fight the urge to tell the driver to turn around, to take me anywhere but there.

As we approached the house, I noticed a small group of people standing on the sidewalk just outside the gates. Paparazzi. My stomach dropped. They were waiting for us, cameras in hand, ready to capture the first images of the famous author and his wife returning home after their bizarre ordeal. The thought of those photographs, of my face splashed across tabloids and websites, made me feel sick.

"Great," Michael muttered under his breath, his hand tightening on my knee. "Just what we need. They already got me when I got out of the hospital, so I didn't think they would be back. Sorry, babe."

"Don't worry," the driver said, "this vehicle has a limo tint that blocks ninety-five percent of visible light. They can't see inside unless they press their nose on the glass."

I felt relieved that Michael had decided to hire a driver for the ride home.

Michael pressed the button on his phone app, and the driveway gate opened. As soon as he had clearance, the driver eased the SUV up the long driveway, and the gate closed, leaving the photographers with nothing to shoot.

The driver drove up to the front door of the house. He quickly got out and opened the door for me. I was moving very slowly, so it took me a hot minute to climb out of the big SUV. Michael exited from the other side of the vehicle, came around to my side and was there, behind the driver, offering his hand to me.

I hesitated, my heart pounding. I didn't want to take his hand. I wanted to trust him and still couldn't, but I didn't want to make things worse, so I took a deep breath and forced myself to reach out and take his hand. His grip was firm, strong. As he helped me out of the car, the sound of the door closing behind me was like the toll of a bell. He helped me onto the pathway leading up to the front door.

"How are you feeling?" Michael asked me.

I couldn't speak. My throat felt tight, my mouth dry. I just wanted to disappear, to melt into the ground and escape from all of this. Michael's hand tightened around mine, and he began to lead me toward the front door.

Each step fell heavier than the last, my legs trembling under the weight of my dread. The pain in my ribs flared at my movements, a sharp reminder of the damage that had been done to my physical body. It had been a patchwork of injuries — broken ribs, a concussion, the gunshot wound that had nearly ended my life — and every step was like a battle against the remnants of that trauma.

I could feel the stitches pulling at my skin, the dull ache in my side reminding me of how close I had come to not making it out alive.

"Melody?" Michael's voice broke through my thoughts, and I realized he had stopped walking. He was staring at me, his brow furrowed with concern.

"Are you okay?" he asked, his voice softer now, gentler.

I assented, but I couldn't find my own voice. I wasn't okay; I was far from okay. But I couldn't tell him that. I couldn't tell him that the house — the place that was supposed to be our home, our sanctuary — now felt like a tomb. I couldn't tell him that every step I took toward that front door filled me with a deeper sense of dread.

We reached the front steps and I hesitated, my feet refusing to move. The memories were too strong, too vivid. I could see the doppelgänger in my mind's eye, his cold smile, his calculating eyes. I could feel the terror, the helplessness, the pain. It all came rushing back, overwhelming me, suffocating me.

"We're home. It can be like before," Michael said softly.

I desperately wanted to believe that. My skin prickled with unease as I looked up at the house which had always been warm and welcoming. Now it loomed large over me, sending chills down my spine.

Without warning, the front door flew open, and every muscle in my body seized in fear.

TWENTY-SEVEN

MELODY

THE FEAR AND DREAD I FELT AS THE FRONT DOOR opened quickly dissipated when I heard Dash's bright, young voice — full of life. "Mom!" And for a moment, everything else melted away.

I looked up to see Dash running toward me, his face lit up with pure joy. His brown hair, just like Michael's, bounced as he sprinted across the driveway, his small feet kicking up dust behind him. In that moment, all the pain, all the fear, seemed to melt away, replaced by a rush of love so powerful it almost knocked me off my feet.

"Dash," I whispered, my voice choked with emotion.

He was nearly upon me now, his arms outstretched, ready to throw himself into my embrace. But before he could reach me, I heard my mother say with sharp concern. "Dash, wait! Be careful!"

"Dash, honey, slow down!" Jessica called out.

"Give your mom some space, Dash," Michael added, his tone gentle but firm.

Dash skidded to a halt just a few feet in front of me, his excitement barely contained. He looked up at me with those big, expressive eyes, so full of love and relief. "Mom, you're home!"

"I am, sweetheart," I said, trying to keep steady as tears welled up in my eyes. "But you have to be gentle with me, okay?"

He nodded vigorously, his eyes wide with understanding. But even as he nodded, I could see the barely contained energy, the desperate need to hug me, to touch me, to know that I was really there, that I was okay. I opened my arms to him, and he stepped forward slowly, carefully, like he was afraid he might hurt me.

His small body pressed against mine, and I bit back a wince. But the pain was nothing compared to the relief of holding him again, of knowing I'd survived and could be here for him.

"I missed you so much," Dash whispered into my chest, his voice trembling.

"I missed you too, baby," I murmured, my voice thick with tears. "So much."

For a moment, the world seemed to fade away, leaving just the two of us, wrapped up in each other. But then I felt a hand on my shoulder, and I looked up to see my mother standing beside me, her eyes red from crying.

"Let's get you inside, Melody," she said.

I reluctantly let go of Dash. He stepped back, looking up at me with a mix of happiness and worry. I could see the questions in his eyes, the unspoken fears he was too young to fully understand. But I couldn't think about that now. I needed to keep moving.

Michael reached for my hand as we walked inside. His hand felt familiar, but something in my chest tightened. Was this really him?

Jessica and Taylor hovered nearby, the same concern etched in their faces. They had been my rocks through all of this, their strength and support giving me the will to keep fighting. Now they watched me with worried eyes, as if they were afraid I might collapse at any moment.

"Take it slow, okay?" Jessica said.

"I'm fine," I replied, though the effort of speaking made me wince. I took another step, and then another, each a small victory over the pain that radiated through my body.

Dash kept close by my side, his hand gently holding mine as if he was afraid to let go. I squeezed his hand, drawing strength from his presence, from the love that flowed between us.

But that feeling of dread returned. I paused, my breath catching in my throat. The memories of that night, of the terror I had endured, rushed back with brutal force. I could see the dark hallways, the looming figure of the doppelgänger, the coldness in his eyes as he taunted me. My knees buckled slightly at the memory of running out of the house, the most scared I'd ever been in my life. Falling into the bunker, seeing Michael chained up... I forced myself to stay upright, to keep moving forward.

"Mom?" Dash's voice pulled me back to the present, his small hand squeezing mine. "Are you okay?"

"I'm okay, Dash," I said, forcing a smile. "I'm just... a little tired, that's all."

He looked at me with those big, trusting eyes, and I knew I couldn't let him see my fear. I had to be strong for him, even if every step seemed to be taking me closer to the edge of a precipice.

My mother stepped up, slipping her arm around my waist to steady me. "We're here with you, Melody," she said softly. "You're not alone."

I nodded, grateful for her support, for all their support. Together we took the final steps up to the door,

Michael reached out and I went inside. As the door opened, I felt a rush of cool air, the familiar scent of our home greeting me. But it didn't feel like home. Not anymore. Michael was right. We had to sell this house. *I can't live here anymore.*

The hallway was dimly lit, the shadows long and deep, stretching before us like a dark tunnel. I hesitated, my heart pounding, but then Dash tugged gently on my hand, pulling me forward.

"Come on, Mom," he said, bright with hope. "It's going to be okay."

As we moved deeper into the house, I could feel the tension in my body easing slightly. The presence of my family and friends was a comforting balm to my frayed nerves, but the shadows still lurked at the edges of my vision, the memories whispering in the back of my mind.

Michael closed the door behind us, sealing us inside. I glanced over at him, searching his face for something — reassurance, familiarity, anything to tell me that this was really my husband, that I wasn't making a terrible mistake.

He met my gaze and smiled, but there was something in his eyes, something that made my heart skip a beat. I quickly looked away, focusing on Dash, on the warmth of his hand in mine.

"Are you okay, Mom?"

"We're going to be okay," I whispered, more to myself than to anyone else.

TWENTY-EIGHT
MELODY

The first week back home passed in a blur, almost too quickly for me to process. Mom, Jessica, and Taylor had returned to Modesto. I could have gone with them, escaped to some semblance of normalcy, but I stayed. I stayed because I had to — because someone needed to pick up the pieces to get our life back to what it was before this nightmare.

Michael seemed to be faring much better than me. It was astonishing, really. This was a man who had been held in an underground bunker, chained by the neck for fifty-eight days, forced to endure unspeakable horrors. His closest friend and agent of seventeen years had been brutally murdered. We had both come within inches of losing our own lives, and in the end, Michael had taken a life. The police had ruled Irvin Skaggs's death as self-defense and justifiable homicide and, of course, I agreed. If it had been me, I would have killed that son of a bitch without hesitation.

But, justifiably or not, Michael had killed a human being. Yet none of that seemed to weigh on him as heavily as it did on me. And I hadn't killed anyone.

My suspicious mind wouldn't stop churning, but I tried to convince myself that I was just being paranoid. Maybe Michael was just stronger than I was, more resilient, better at compartmentalizing the trauma that had nearly destroyed us both.

Despite my dark thoughts, every day I felt a little better. I started eating again now that the antibiotics had been flushed out of my system. I gradually reduced my pain medication, tapering down to just one pill every other day. The last thing I needed was to trade one problem for another, to develop an opiate addiction on top of everything else.

Michael had returned to his writing, holed up in his office for hours at a time. The publisher had canceled the contract he had been working under and told him to take his time, to write without deadlines or pressure. Not that it mattered much; the vultures had already started circling before Lydia's body was even cold in the ground, agents from all over reaching out to Michael, eager to represent him, to be a part of the next chapter in his storied career. "Do I even need an agent anymore?" he had asked me one night, a distant look in his eyes.

The publisher had begun planting the seed for Michael's first nonfiction book, dangling an eight-figure advance as incentive. It was to be a true crime story, based on what we had gone through. They even had a title picked out for him: *The Doppelgänger*.

The very thought of it made me sick. The idea of turning our nightmare into entertainment for the masses, of having every painful detail laid bare for public consumption — it was too much. Michael was still banged up, even if he'd managed to ditch the cane, and we hadn't even tried to be intimate since the ordeal, something I was secretly relieved about. Nothing kills your libido like almost sleeping with a deranged killer posing as your husband who then tries to kill you.

This morning, Michael had gone out to meet with one of the agents who had flown in from New York to sweet talk him into signing with his agency. He'd been hesitant to leave me alone with Dash, but I had insisted he go. I was feeling better, almost like myself again, and I didn't want him to worry. He'd promised to only be gone for a couple of hours. I told him not to worry about me.

But as soon as he left, a part of me felt a guilty sense of relief. I was alone — really alone for the first time since I had come home — and I knew exactly what I needed to do. I had to know, once and for all, if I was really living with my husband or if the man who had returned with me was still someone else, someone dangerous. I headed outside.

Every step toward his office sent a sharp ache through my ribs, a reminder of how broken I still was, physically and mentally. I forced myself not to look at the part of the backyard with the entrance to the bunker, but I could feel its presence, lurking like a shadow in the corner of my vision. I had told Michael I would never set foot near there again. It was one of the reasons I had finally agreed to sell the house. There were too many painful memories that would linger long after my body had healed.

When I finally reached the office, I hesitated at the door, my hand trembling as I reached for the knob. I felt a wave of disgust wash over me — disgust at myself for snooping, for doubting Michael. But it wasn't enough to stop me. I needed to know the truth, whatever that truth might be. I stepped inside.

Everything was neat, orderly. Nothing seemed out of place. Not sure what I was expecting to see. But I couldn't shake the feeling that something was wrong. His computer was locked, as I'd expected, so I entered the password he had always shared with me. "Just in case I get hit by a bus," he used to joke, back when death was a distant, abstract concept, not the all-too-real specter it had become in our lives. But the field jumped, and a warning appeared: "Incorrect password." I tried again, my hands trembling, but got the same result. He had changed the password and not told me. I didn't dare try a third time for fear of locking it completely.

I sat for a moment at his desk, feeling the weight of my suspicion bearing down on me. Everything about the room was designed to minimize distractions — bare walls, no clutter, no personal touches beyond the framed covers of his previous novels on the walls. The desk didn't even have drawers, and as I scanned the room, the bile rose in my throat at the betrayal I was committing.

I was a fool, chasing shadows in my own home. Suspicious of my husband, who had also gone through hell and back in the hands of Irvin Skaggs.

I was about to leave, about to put all that madness behind me, when something caught my eye — a piece of fabric, barely visible behind some books on the shelf. It was so out of place, so foreign to the spartan nature of Michael's workspace, that it immediately grabbed my attention. My heart began to race as I walked over to the bookshelf, my steps faltering, my breath coming in short, panicked bursts.

I stood frozen, staring at the shelf, at the edge of the fabric peeking out. My fingers hovered in the air, uncertain, as if touching it would make the nightmare real. The fabric seemed to be hidden behind several books. I reached out with trembling fingers, pulling back the thick, weighty volumes seemingly used to hide something — Tolkien, Michener, Follett — until I could see what was hidden behind them. I recognized it right away. It was one of our kitchen towels, which he had used to wrap around something bulky, something he wanted to hide.

My hands were sweaty, shaking as I reached for it, my heart pounding in my ears. Did I really want to see what he was hiding?

TWENTY-NINE
MELODY

I STARED AT THE BLACK BAG THAT HAD BEEN wrapped up in our kitchen towel for what felt like an eternity, my mind struggling to make sense of what I was seeing. The clear front of the bag displayed its contents neatly, almost innocently, as if it were just another ordinary item in our home. The bold white text on the bag read *All-Pro Makeup Kit*, and for a moment, I felt a sense of relief wash over me. Makeup. It's just makeup, I told myself. Maybe there was some simple explanation for why Michael had this, something benign, something that wouldn't send my heart racing or make my stomach churn.

But as I stood there, the initial relief began to erode, replaced by a gnawing sense of dread. Why would Michael have a makeup kit like this? And why was he hiding it from me? My hands trembled violently as I zipped open the bag, my breath coming in ragged gasps. The sight of the prosthetics, the fake blood — it was all too much. My stomach did churn, and I had to fight the urge to vomit right there in Michael's office.

This wasn't ordinary makeup. This was a professional special-effects kit — something used by makeup artists in Hollywood to create realistic wounds, scars, and other grotesque effects for movies and television shows.

My breath caught in my throat as I unzipped another pouch inside the bag. Inside, I found a palette branded as *SFX Colors*, with a range of sickly, unnatural hues that could be used to create bruises, burns, and other effects to recreate wounds. As I dug deeper into the kit, I found a round tin can that looked like it might contain shoe polish, but the label read *Scar Wax*. I opened the tin, revealing a pale, flesh-colored substance that could be molded and shaped into realistic scars. My hands shook as I put the tin back and reached for the last item in the bag — a booklet, worn and dog-eared, with the words *Special FX Makeup: Techniques and Tutorials* printed across the front.

I flipped through the booklet, each page making my heart pound harder. There were detailed instructions on how to create a variety of effects, everything from simple bruises to complex, layered prosthetics. My eyes scanned the pages, and I found an entire section dedicated to creating realistic-looking scars. The images, so lifelike, so grotesque, made my skin crawl.

I couldn't believe what I was seeing. The scar Michael had shown me that day in the hospital, the one I had demanded to see, the one that had given me a moment of peace, a moment when I believed that I was safe, that I was with my real husband. But now, staring down at this special-effects kit, at the instructions on how to create scars that looked convincingly real, a wave of nausea rose in my throat. The scar Michael had shown me had to be fake. Created with this kit.

The blood drained from my face, my vision narrowing as panic threatened to overwhelm me. My breaths came in short, shallow gasps, my mind racing with the implications of what I had discovered. Tears welled up in my eyes, but I forced them back. I couldn't break down now. I needed to think, needed to figure out what to do next. My hands trembled as I reached into my pocket and pulled out my phone. I snapped several photographs of the kit, making sure to capture the labels, the prosthetics, the booklet — everything. I needed proof. Proof that I wasn't going crazy, that I wasn't just being paranoid.

With the photos taken, I began to carefully put everything back in the bag, wrapping it up in the towel as if I hadn't found it and gone through its contents. My fingers fumbled as I tried to shove the bag back behind the books. I kept glancing over my shoulder, half expecting Michael to appear in the doorway, his dark eyes watching me with that strange, unreadable expression.

Finally, I managed to get everything back in place. I straightened the books, making sure they were aligned just as they had been before. I couldn't let him know that I had found his secret. Not yet.

I turned to leave the office, my legs feeling weak and unsteady beneath me. Each step felt like a monumental effort, my mind reeling from the revelation. I needed to get out of here, needed to get back to the house, needed to think. But as I reached the door, my hand paused on the knob, a cold chill running down my spine.

If the man who had brought me home wasn't Michael, then where was my real husband? Was he still out there somewhere, alive? Back in that bunker? Or was he dead, buried in some unmarked grave, while this imposter took his place, stole his life all over again. And again, I had been easily hoodwinked. What the hell was wrong with me?

My breath was labored; I felt a panic attack rising, so I squeezed my eyes shut, trying to block out the horrifying images that flashed through my mind. I couldn't let myself think like that. I had to stay focused, had to stay calm. I opened the door and stepped outside, the cool air hitting my face like a splash of water. I took a deep breath, steadying myself, pushing back the tide of panic. I had to act normal. I couldn't let him suspect that I knew.

I made my way back to the main house, my steps slow and deliberate. When I reached the front door, I paused, my hand hovering over the handle. Inside, Dash was waiting for me, innocent and unaware of the danger that lurked so close. I had to protect him. I had to protect myself.

I pushed open the door and stepped inside, the warmth of the house enveloping me. But it didn't feel like home anymore. It felt like a trap, like a place where darkness and secrets festered, waiting to consume us.

I heard footsteps behind me and turned to see Michael standing at the top of the stairs, looking down at me with that same inscrutable expression. His eyes were dark, unreadable, and I couldn't shake the feeling that he knew that I had been snooping in his writing office.

"I couldn't find you, I got worried," he said, his voice smooth, calm, almost taunting. The way he spoke sent a shiver down my spine, like cold fingers trailing along my skin.

My heart skipped a beat and I forced a smile, my mind racing as I tried to come up with a response. But the words caught in my throat, and all I could do was stare up at him, fear clawing at my insides, threatening to pull me under.

"I was out on the patio, getting some fresh air," I said, trying to sound normal. "How was your meeting? Did you like the agent?" I asked, desperate to steer the conversation away from where I had been and what I had found.

He smiled, but something was off about him. "He

was okay. Promising me the world on a silver platter, of course."

I nodded, keeping the conversation light, as if everything were perfectly normal. "Well, good spot to be in, all these top agents fighting for you."

But his smile faded, replaced by a cold, hard look that sent my heart into a tailspin. "They're just liars. I hate liars," he said, the words dripping with an icy disdain that made my blood run cold.

He started down the stairs, each step deliberate, measured, as if he were savoring the tension in the air. My hands clenched into fists at my sides as I watched him approach, every instinct screaming at me to run, to get out, to protect myself and Dash.

As Michael reached the bottom of the stairs he moved toward me and his smile grew wider, but it wasn't a smile of warmth or comfort. It made me shiver.

"I picked up dinner. Let's eat," he said, his tone smooth, casual, as if we were just a normal couple talking about their day. But the way he said it, the way his eyes bore into mine, sent a fresh wave of panic coursing through me.

I swallowed hard, my throat dry. "Sure," I managed to say, though my voice sounded distant, like it belonged to someone else. I couldn't let him see how terrified I was, couldn't let him know that I had discovered his secret.

He reached out and placed a hand on my shoulder,

his grip firm, almost too firm. The touch made me flinch, but I forced myself to stay still, to keep my composure. His eyes never left mine, and I could feel the weight of his gaze, the way it seemed to strip away the layers of my defenses, exposing every fear, every doubt.

"Melody," he said softly with something I couldn't quite place — was it concern? Mockery? It was impossible to tell. "You seem tense. Is everything okay?"

The question hung in the air, thick with meaning. I could feel the walls closing in around me, the floor shifting beneath my feet. I had to play this carefully, had to keep him from suspecting that I was onto him.

"I'm just tired," I said, forcing a weary smile. "It's been a long day."

His eyes narrowed slightly, as if he didn't quite believe me, but then he released my shoulder and stepped back. "Of course. You've been through a lot. We both have."

He turned and walked toward the kitchen, leaving me there. I had to get a grip, had to keep it together. I couldn't afford to let my fear show, not now. Not when everything was at stake.

I followed him into the kitchen, the familiar space now feeling alien, threatening. The table was set with takeout containers, the aroma of food filling the room, but I couldn't even think about eating. My stomach was in knots, my thoughts spinning out of control.

Michael gestured for me to sit and I complied, my

movements stiff and mechanical. He sat across from me, his eyes never leaving my face as he began to unpack the food. I tried to focus, to act normal, but all I could think about was the special-effects kit, the scar wax, the fake blood. The image of that fake nose, so lifelike in its detail, haunted me, reminding me that the man sitting across from me might not be who he claimed to be.

"Everything looks great," I said, though the words felt hollow, forced.

He smiled again, that same unsettling smile, and began to serve the food. "I thought you might like some comfort food," he said airily. "Something to help us both feel a little more normal."

Normal. The word echoed in my mind, mocking me. There was nothing normal about this situation, nothing normal about the fear that gripped me every time I looked at him.

I forced myself to take a bite, the food tasteless in my mouth. I chewed mechanically, my mind racing with questions, with doubts. Was he playing with me? Did he know that I had been in his office, that I had found the makeup kit? Or was he just testing me, seeing how far he could push before I broke?

As we ate in silence, I couldn't shake the feeling that I was being watched, scrutinized. Every glance, every word felt like a trap, like a test that I couldn't afford to fail. And as the meal dragged on, the tension in the air grew thicker, suffocating.

Finally, I couldn't take it anymore. I pushed my plate away, my appetite gone. "I think I'm going to go to bed," I said, standing up, trembling slightly.

Michael looked up at me, his eyes narrowing just a fraction. "So early? You haven't eaten much."

"I'm just really tired," I said, forcing another smile. "I'll feel better after a good night's sleep."

He watched me for a moment and I held my breath, praying that he wouldn't press the issue, that he would let me leave. Then, slowly, he nodded. "Of course. You need your rest."

Relief flooded through me, but it was short-lived. As I turned to leave, he stopped me in my tracks.

"Melody?"

I froze, my hand on the doorframe. "Yes?"

"Don't go sneaking around anymore," he said, his voice low, dangerous. "It's not safe."

My blood ran cold, and I turned to look at him. His eyes were dark, intense, and there was no mistaking the threat in his words.

"I—I wasn't—" I stammered, but he cut me off with a sharp smile.

"Goodnight, Melody," he said dismissively. The conversation was over.

THIRTY
MELODY

BY THE MORNING, I HAD BEGUN TO QUESTION WHY I had freaked out. Michael was a writer. He was always researching weird stuff for his books. I can't recall how many times I glanced over at his computer when he was doing research to see something horrific on the screen like photographs of bloody crime scenes and autopsies. And searches like *how to torture someone by pulling out the fingernails*. I'd seen it all. And it was a humorous topic of conversation during dinner parties with friends. It was part of living with a writer of thrillers.

I was letting my imagination run wild and allowing it to think the worst, instead of applying common sense and logic. The police closed the case. The detective and forensic investigators spent days at our property. They found two dead bodies here, Lydia and Irvin Skaggs. They determined that Skaggs killed Lydia, and

Michael killed Irvin Skaggs in self-defense. The police ran all sorts of tests. DNA stuff. Skaggs might be able to fool me, but not the police. I could ask him about things that I knew only Michael would know about, but going that route felt like I was playing with fire. I was afraid about what he would do if I were to do that.

I felt like my head was getting scrambled with all these dark thoughts and suspicions about my husband, so I called Dr. Kanzaria who had told me I could reach out anytime if I needed to talk.

He listened and then calmly and kindly he said: "You've gone through an incredible traumatic event in your life, Melody. And please allow me to remind you, all this occurred very recently. So this trauma is still very fresh and you're still processing everything that happened to you. It's not uncommon for survivors of violent crime to struggle with their footing afterwards. Victims' physical wounds recover much faster than the mental ones. So your feelings of being unsafe, suspicions about your husband's behavior, finding a makeup kit and thinking the worst of it, this is all normal. You're probably dealing with symptoms of PTSD as well."

"So I'm going crazy?"

"Crazy is not a word I ever use in my practice. PTSD is very real. And it's something I can help you manage. Talking about what we're doing now will be of benefit for you. There are medications to help you control the PTSD. I'll have my admin reach out to set up appointments for you. I think we should meet weekly for the next few months."

"Okay," I said.

"And Melody, you have to cut your husband some slack. He too is probably dealing with the emotional trauma of what has happened. Being held captive in an underground bunker for months. Watching you get shot. Killing a man. His PTSD could be very bad, which is why he is acting strange."

I felt like a heel, so worried about how I was dealing with all this and not putting much stock on what Michael might be going through.

I hung up. Despite what the doctor had just said and his reassurances, I couldn't help but think that I was going fucking crazy. So I told Michael I was going to visit my mother. He worried about me driving all the way to Modesto, as I was still recovering, but I reassured him I felt better and stronger every day. It was only a ninety-minute drive if I avoided rush hour, and a trip I'd made so often I could do it blindfolded. So he reluctantly saw me off.

"What are you going to do while I'm gone?" I asked him.

"Work on my book."

"How's it going?"

"Good. I'm locked in, so I'm happy about that."

"What's it about?"

"One of the best special FX artists in Hollywood begins to lose his mind."

I drove to Modesto and dropped Dash off with my mother. She was happy to watch him for a few days, but she worried about me. I didn't tell her of my suspicions or about finding the makeup kit; after talking with Dr. Kanzaria and finding out that Michael's character was an FX artist, I thought I had let my mind run way too wild. But still, I needed to figure things out, and I didn't want to worry about Dash's safety.

Maybe it was staying at that house. *We should rent somewhere else and just sell that damned house. A change of scenery would be nice. Palm Springs. Napa perhaps.*

As I drove back to the city, I wanted to discuss all this with Michael. After I got out of the hospital, we hadn't really talked about what he had gone through; he was busy with his book and getting his business affairs in order now that Lydia was gone.

But despite everything I was trying to do to not let my paranoia take over me, it still crept back. So even though I felt guilt, I kept the appointment I had made with Inspector Ganns right after I found the makeup kit.

I went to the Philz Coffee Shop near the ballpark and he was there.

"Thank you so much for meeting with me."

"No problem, Mrs. Reed. What can I do for you?"

I told him about how I was struggling to get back to

my normal life which the crimes of Irvin Skaggs had torn apart. And how I still sometimes doubted that he was dead. And I showed him the pictures I took of the special FX makeup kit, including a close shot of the makeup to create scars and wounds.

Ganns sipped his coffee, taking it all in.

"Mrs. Reed, what you went through, I can't even fathom. Living with someone whom you thought was your husband when he wasn't, well, I'm sure that's a lot to have to work through. But the case is closed. The dead man in that bunker was Irvin Skaggs."

"So you did the DNA testing and it confirmed that was Skaggs?"

Ganns shifted in his chair.

"We took the DNA samples and sent it to the lab, but the lab is backed up and this is a low priority case since it's been closed, so we won't get the official results for several months. Might be a year."

"A year?" I said in disbelief.

Ganns smiled, as if he was used to getting this reaction from victims and family members of cases he's worked on. "Unfortunately in real police work these things take time. It's not like on television and the movies, when they get DNA results instantly."

"There is no way of speeding up the process?"

"Even if there was compelling evidence that warranted bumping it up, we would still be talking about weeks if not a month or two. You would need a push like from the mayor perhaps to get faster than that. From where I stand, I don't see anything here that would require trying to speed up the process. You husband makes up stories for a living and you said yourself he does a lot of research. So I wouldn't put too much stock on that makeup kit. And we have conducted a thorough investigation. I'm certain the dead man in that bunker was Irvin Skaggs."

"You mentioned at the hospital that my husband wasn't cooperating. Did he finally sit down with you to discuss things?" I asked.

"Quite the opposite. He got one of the top trial lawyers in the state to do the talking for him. The lawyer said your husband is too traumatized to sit down for an in-depth interview. So we got the basics through the lawyer."

"Isn't that strange?" I asked.

"Not when it comes to rich and connected people, Mrs. Reed. They usually let the lawyers do the talking, and that's within their rights. I can't force him to sit down and talk to me without evidence and there is nothing to change that. So we had enough to work the case and close it."

Ganns must have noticed the look of disappointment in my face.

"Listen, Mrs. Reed, you're a wealthy person. So if you want to speed up things independently, you can do so privately."

"What do you mean?" Ganns reached into his coat and removed a pocket notebook from it. He took out a pen and as he wrote in it, he said, "This is the number for Dexter Mills. He was my partner before Sanchez. He retired from the SFPD three years ago and is now a private investigator. If I ever needed someone to look into things for me privately, I would hire Dexter. He's a hell of an investigator." Ganns tore off the sheet of paper from his notebook and handed it to me.

"I don't think you have anything to worry about, Mrs. Reed, but if you need a bit more reassurance than I can offer officially, then Dexter is your man."

THIRTY-ONE
MELODY

DEXTER MILLS'S OFFICE WAS LOCATED DOWNTOWN on Ellis Street in a building next to the famous restaurant John's Grill. I stood on the sidewalk as my gaze drifted to the sign above the entrance of the restaurant. The iconic green and white lettering was a reminder of the restaurant's rich history, steeped in the lore of classic detective fiction.

I couldn't help but think of the countless times Michael had talked about Dashiell Hammett, his eyes lighting up as he recounted stories about the author's gritty characters and twisting plots. It was one of the reasons he'd insisted on naming our son Dashiell — after one of the great writers of crime fiction.

The irony of it all struck me like a punch to the gut. Here I was, standing on the same street where one of Michael's literary heroes had once walked, about to step into a private investigator's office to find out whether the man I was married to was even my husband at all; whether the twisted plot around me could be unraveled. Except that this wasn't the plot of a novel. It was my life that was at stake. Or, at the very least, my mental sanity.

I took a deep breath, trying to steady myself, but my nerves were frayed, and I could feel the anxiety bubbling up inside me, threatening to spill over. I clenched my fists, my nails digging into my palms as I forced myself to focus. I couldn't afford to fall apart now. I had to see this through, for my sake, for Dash's.

I went into the building. There was a security guard manning the entrance.

"May I help you?"

I told him I had an appointment with Dexter Mills, embarrassed that I should be looking for a private investigator.

"Eighth floor, suite 816," he said without judgment as he pointed back towards the elevators.

The building was old and dated. I rode the creaky elevator up, and I couldn't shake the feeling that I was walking into a scene straight out of a noir novel. The kind of scene where the heroine finds herself on the brink of discovering something that will change her life forever — something she's not sure she wants to know.

The elevator doors slid open with a groan, and I stepped out into a narrow hallway covered with a faded carpet. The muted sound of jazz music drifted from one of the offices, mingling with the distant hum of city traffic outside. I walked slowly, looking at the numbers on the doors until I reached the one I was looking for: 816. There was a small placard on it that said, *Dexter Mills Private Investigative Services.*

I had googled Dexter Mills after I called to make an appointment. His credentials were impressive, his client reviews glowing, and he had a reputation for discretion that had sealed the deal. I needed someone who wouldn't ask too many questions, someone who wouldn't judge me for the paranoia that had taken root in my mind. But I also needed him to be discreet because the vultures of the entertainment press found out that I had a private investigator looking into Michael. It would be big news on the gossip sites.

My heart pounded as I thought about all that, my hand hovering over the door handle. Was I about to blow up my life based on a gut feeling, a paranoia I couldn't shake? But what if I was right?

And what if I was wrong, and this was all just the result of my own fractured psyche struggling to make sense of the trauma we'd been through, just as my psychiatrist had said? Ganns hadn't taken my concerns seriously. If the police could close the case, why couldn't I?

What if I was about to tear my life even further apart for nothing?

I would have walked away, but instead I shook my head, pushing those thoughts aside. I couldn't afford to second-guess myself. The stakes were too high, so I opened the door and stepped inside.

The office was small, cluttered but not messy, with stacks of papers and manila folders covering almost every surface. The walls were adorned with old black-and-white photographs of San Francisco, celebrating a bygone era of the City by the Bay.

It was a one-man office. A large wooden desk dominated the room, behind which sat Dexter Mills.

He didn't look much different than the picture he had of himself on his website, maybe a tad older now. He was in his late fifties, with thinning gray hair slicked back from a high forehead. He dressed casually, like he was about to go golfing. Mills had the look of someone who had seen it all, and then some.

But it was his eyes that caught my attention the most. Sharp, blue, and observant. He studied me as I walked in, his gaze assessing, taking in every detail, every nuance of my body language.

I felt exposed under his scrutiny, as if he could see right through me, see the fear and doubt that had brought me here.

"Mrs. Reed, I presume?" he said, standing up and extending his hand.

"Yes," I replied, my voice a little shaky as I reached out. His grip was firm, reassuring.

"Please, have a seat," he said, gesturing to the chair in front of his desk.

I sat down, feeling the worn leather creak beneath

me. The chair was surprisingly comfortable, and I settled into it, trying to steady my nerves. Mills sat back down, folding his hands on the desk in front of him, and leaned forward slightly, giving me his full attention.

"What can I do for you, Mrs. Reed?" he asked, his manner calm and professional.

I hesitated, my mind racing as I tried to figure out how to start. How do you explain to someone that you think your husband might not be your husband? That the man you've been living with, the man you've shared a life with, might be an imposter?

"I—" I began, then paused, swallowing hard. "I need you to investigate someone for me."

Mills's expression was patient as he waited for me to continue.

"It's… it's my husband," I said, the words feeling foreign and strange as they left my mouth.

"You suspect an affair?"

"No. I wish it were that simple."

Mills looked at me in surprise. I had caught the grizzled detective off guard.

"I think something's wrong with him. I think… I think he might not be who he says he is."

There it was, out in the open. The thing that had been gnawing at me for weeks, the fear that had taken hold of my heart and refused to let go. I watched Mill's reaction carefully, looking for any sign that he thought I was crazy, that he was about to dismiss me as some paranoid wife with an overactive imagination.

But he didn't. He simply nodded, as if this was the most normal request in the world.

"Tell me more," he said, his tone steady, encouraging.

I took a deep breath and started from the beginning, telling him about everything that had happened — the kidnapping, the underground bunker, the murder of Skaggs, and the nightmare that had followed us home. I told him about the special effects kit I had found, about the scar I was now convinced was fake, and about the strange behavior that had made me question everything I thought I knew about Michael.

As I spoke, Mills listened intently, never interrupting, his eyes never leaving my face. He didn't take notes, didn't ask for clarification. He just listened, absorbing every word, every detail. It felt strange, talking about all of this to a stranger, but at the same time, it was a relief — a weight lifted off my shoulders. It felt even more therapeutic than my sessions with Dr. Kanzaria.

When I finished, there was a long silence. Mill leaned back in his chair, his fingers steepled in front of him as he considered what I had said. The jazz music from down the hall was just audible in the background, a soothing, melancholy tune that seemed at odds with the tension in the room.

Finally, he spoke. "Mrs. Reed, what you're

describing is... unusual, to say the least. But I'm aware of your unique circumstances. I followed it on the news, and the police closed the case. But I want you to know that I take all my clients' concerns seriously. If you believe there's something wrong despite all that, then I'm here to help you find the truth."

His words were a balm to my frayed nerves, a promise that I wasn't alone in this, that someone else was on my side. But they were also a reminder that finding the truth could mean unraveling my entire life, tearing down everything I thought I knew.

"What do you want me to do?" he asked gently, as if sensing the turmoil inside me.

I hesitated, the enormity of the situation crashing down. I was standing at the edge of a precipice, and once I took that first step, there would be no turning back.

"I need to know," I finally said, my voice barely above a whisper. "I need to know if the man I'm living with is really my husband... or if he's someone else."

Mills nodded gravely. "I can do that for you. I'll start right away, if that's what you want."

"It is," I said softly.

"Okay. I'll need as much information as you can provide — everything you know about your husband, his habits, his routines, any of these changes you've noticed. All of them. Big and small."

I reached into my bag and pulled out a folder I had prepared, filled with copies of Michael's documents, photos, and notes I had made over the past few weeks. My hands shook slightly as I handed it to him, the weight of what I was doing sinking in.

He took the folder, his expression unreadable as he flipped through the contents. "This will help," he said, setting it aside. "Give me a few days. I'll keep you updated on my progress. In the meantime, if you notice anything else, anything at all, don't hesitate to contact me 24/7," he said. He handed me a business card. "That's my private card, for clients only. It has all the ways you can reach me directly."

I took the card, feeling a mixture of fear and relief. Fear of what he might find, and relief that I wasn't facing this alone.

As I stood to leave, Mills rose from his chair and walked me to the door. "Take care of yourself, Mrs. Reed," he said, his tone kind, almost fatherly. "And remember — you're doing the right thing for peace of mind."

I nodded, though I wasn't sure I believed him. As I stepped out into the hallway, the weight of my decision pressed down on me like a heavy blanket. What had I just done?

THIRTY-TWO
MICHAEL

MELODY LIVED IN FEAR OF ME. I COULD SEE IT IN the way she flinched when I got too close, the way her eyes darted away whenever I tried to meet them, searching for the warmth that used to be there just a few months ago. It was gone, replaced by something dark and wary. I didn't know what more I needed to do to make her trust me.

Dr. Kanzaria said it was going to be a long, hard slog for both of us — rebuilding what had been shattered between us, piecing together the remnants of our lives after the horror we'd been through. But as each day passed, I began to wonder if it was even possible. If Melody would ever see me as the man she had once loved, or if she would always look at me and see... someone else.

I tried to be patient. To give her space. I understood that what we'd been through wasn't something you just "get over." The scars we carried weren't just physical. They went deeper than that, cutting into the very essence of who we were in our souls.

But I couldn't help but feel a gnawing frustration, a creeping sense of helplessness that made me question everything. What else could I do? How much longer could I endure this? When was she going to snap out of it?

The doctor had said it might take months, even years, to rebuild the trust that had been eroded, to reclaim the sense of safety and normalcy that had been stolen from us. Years? *I can't go on for years like this, that's for sure.* Whenever I thought Melody was coming around, I looked into her eyes — if she was not avoiding mine — and what I saw made me believe that what our life together was beyond repair.

She tried to hide it, but I could see the suspicion lurking there, the questions she was too afraid to ask.

I knew what she wanted to know. Was I really her husband? Was I really the man who had shared her life, her bed, her dreams for years before the imposter tried to take it all away? Or was I something else, something dark and twisted, masquerading as the man she once knew?

It hurt, more than I cared to admit. The idea that she could look at me and not know, not be certain. But what hurt more was the doubt that had started to creep into my own mind. The questions that had begun to keep me up late at night.

Was I really Michael Reed?

I shook off that thought as soon as it entered my mind. *Of course I'm me.* I had memories of our first vacation together, of our wedding day, but lately even those seemed to blur at the edges, as if I had learned about those memories from an old photograph or a video, not as if I had lived them.

Melody wasn't making it easy for me with her doubts. Now when I looked in the mirror and didn't recognize the man staring back at me. At some moments, I felt like a stranger in my own skin.

It wasn't supposed to be like this. We were supposed to be healing, moving forward. But every time I reached out to Melody, every time I tried to bridge the gap that had opened between us, I could feel her pulling away, retreating further into herself, into her fear. And that fear was contagious. It spread through our house like a virus, infecting every corner, every interaction. I could feel it seeping into me, twisting my thoughts, making me question everything.

I wasn't sure how much longer I could do this. How much longer I could live in this house, in this life, where every day felt like a test I was bound to fail. Where every word, every gesture, was scrutinized, dissected, analyzed for hidden meaning by Melody.

I had to find a way to fix this. To prove to Melody that I was who I said I was. That I wasn't... him.

But how do you prove something like that? How do you make someone believe in you again when the very fabric of your identity has been called into question? How do you convince someone that you're real when they can't even look at you without seeing a ghost?

I walked through the house, my footsteps echoing in the silence. The walls seemed to be closing in, pressing down on me with the weight of all the unspoken doubts and fears that had accumulated over the past weeks. I needed to clear my head, to get out, to escape this oppressive atmosphere that suffocated me.

I stepped outside, the cool evening air washing over me like a balm. The garden was quiet and the flowers swayed gently in the breeze, the world beyond our walls carrying on as if nothing had happened. But here, in our world, everything had changed.

I found myself standing at the edge of the garden, near the door to the shelter as memories came rushing back.

I heard a sound behind me and turned to see Melody standing in the doorway, watching me. Her expression was guarded, her body tense, as if she was ready to bolt at any moment. My heart ached at the sight of her, at the distance between us that felt like an insurmountable chasm.

"Are you okay?" she asked in a whisper.

I nodded, forcing a smile. "Just needed some fresh air," I said, trying to sound casual. I knew she was terrified to come this close to the bunker.

I saw her move forward, but she hesitated then took a tentative step backward into the house. Her eyes searched mine, looking for... what? Reassurance? Answers? Or was she looking for something else, something that would confirm her worst fears? I made my way back to where she stood.

"Melody," I pleaded. "You don't have to be afraid of me."

She didn't respond, didn't move, just stood there, watching me with those haunted eyes, as if she were trying to decide whether to believe me.

I wanted to reach out to her, to close the distance between us, to pull her into my arms and hold her until all the fear and doubt melted away. But I couldn't. I couldn't move, couldn't bring myself to cross that invisible line that had been drawn between us.

"I'm not him," I said, the words slipping out before I could stop them.

Her eyes widened, and I saw the flicker of something in them — was it relief? Doubt? Or something darker?

She opened her mouth to say something, but then closed it again, as if she couldn't find the words. The silence stretched between us, heavy with all the things we weren't saying, all the things we couldn't say.

Finally, she nodded, just once, and turned to go back inside. I watched the door close softly behind her.

I stood there in the gathering darkness, alone with

my thoughts, the doubts, the fears. I was Michael Reed. I had to be. But as the shadows deepened around me, I couldn't shake the feeling that maybe, just maybe, I was losing myself.

THIRTY-THREE
MELODY

Michael's question hung in the air between us, heavy and charged. I could feel my heart pounding in my chest, my breath coming in shallow gasps as I tried to process what he was asking — what he was offering.

He followed me inside.

"What do you need me to do to prove it, Melody?" His voice was soft, but there was an edge to it that sent a shiver down my spine. He closed the distance between us, his eyes locked on mine. "Tell me, and I'll do it."

I swallowed hard, my throat dry.

"I—I want to see the scar," I stammered, barely recognizing the sound of my own voice. "I want to touch it."

For a moment, Michael just stared at me, his expression unreadable. I couldn't tell if he was angry, hurt, or something else entirely. Then, slowly, he nodded, though his jaw tightened, the muscles in his neck tensing as if he were bracing himself for something painful.

"Okay," he said. "Okay, if that's what you need to believe me. Fine."

He pulled his shirt out from the waistband of his jeans and began to unbutton his pants with deliberate, measured movements. I watched, my eyes wide, my breath caught in my throat. My mind was screaming at me to stop this, to turn away, not to go through with it. If it was makeup, what then? Would he kill me? If the scar was real, would Michael ever forgive me for doubting him? For siccing Dexter Mills onto him?

I was willing to deal with those possible consequences. I just needed to know, once and for all, if the man standing in front of me was really Michael Reed — or if he was this Irvin Skaggs, the man who had stolen my husband's face, his life.

Michael lifted his shirt and lowered his pants far enough so I could see it. He turned his head away from me. I saw the scar running diagonally across his abdomen, just as I remembered it.

He turned his head to face me. "Go ahead. Touch it," he said. There was a challenge in his eyes now, as if he were daring me to find something wrong, something that would confirm my suspicions. Or to show me I had gone mad.

My hand trembled as I reached out, my fingers

hovering just above the scar. My heart was racing so fast I thought it might burst from my chest. My mind spun with a thousand possibilities, a thousand fears. This was it. This was the moment of truth.

I took a deep breath and placed my hand on his scar. I wondered if I could smear the makeup. The skin was warm, the texture uneven beneath my fingertips, a mix of smooth and rough. I pressed down gently, feeling the firmness of the scar tissue, the way it pulled slightly as I moved my hand. It was real. It wasn't makeup, it wasn't some elaborate disguise. It was a real scar, a part of him, a part of his body. I pressed it, which made him flinch.

"Still recovering from my own wounds," he said defensively.

The room tilted around me as I tried to make sense of what I felt. Had I been wrong this whole time? Had I let my fear, my trauma, twist my perception of reality? I had talked to Inspector Ganns, I had hired a private investigator, I had done everything I could to find the truth — and, it seemed, the truth had been right in front of me this whole time. And it wasn't the truth I had expected. It wasn't the truth I had feared. It was something else, something that left me reeling, questioning everything I thought I knew and made me ashamed of the way I had been treating Micael.

Warm tears trickled down my cheeks.

"I'm sorry," I whispered, my voice breaking as the

weight of my doubt, my suspicion, came crashing down on me. "I'm so sorry, Michael."

He reached out and gently cupped my face in his hands, his touch warm, his gaze intense. "It's okay," he said softly. "I know you've been through hell. We both have. But I'm here. I'm real. And I'm not going anywhere."

I tried to hold back my tears, but I couldn't. For weeks I had been living in a state of constant fear, doubting the man I had loved, the man I had shared my life with, the father of my only child. And now, in this moment, it all seemed so clear, so painfully obvious.

How could I have been so wrong? How could I have let my fear control me, cloud my judgment, make me doubt the person who had always been there for me? The person who had saved me from Irvin Skaggs, who had fought for me, who had been through hell and back only for me to make him feel like a stranger.

"What have I done?" I said.

"We're going to get through this," he said, his voice steady, reassuring. "Together."

I wanted to tell him about Dexter Mills, but I couldn't. He might not be able to forgive me that much. So I just nodded.

"Thank you," I said. "Thank you for being patient with me."

Michael's smile softened and he pulled me into his arms, holding me close, his warmth enveloping me, grounding me. I let myself relax against him, let myself believe, even if only for a moment, that everything was going to be okay. That I wasn't living in a nightmare, that the man holding me was really my husband, the man I had loved for so long.

But then that feeling came back. Why? Why did I still feel like I was in the arms of a stranger? A feeling that hadn't just vanished at touching the scar.

Stop it, I chided myself.

I squeezed my eyes shut, willing the thoughts away, willing myself to believe that this was real, that this was my life, my husband. But the doubt didn't go away. There was that small, insistent voice that refused to be silenced: *That's not your husband.*

THIRTY-FOUR
MELODY

The next morning, I drove up to Modesto with Dash. I had enrolled him in a young coder's workshop in San Jose, so it would be a few weeks before Mom could see him again. She was grateful I'd brought him up for a visit. I was glad to be away from the house.

I told my mom about the coder camp. "Is that like a summer camp?" she asked.

"Sort of, but not like the ones you sent me on that were basically camping out in the woods with nothing much to do. This camp focuses on learning computer programming versus hanging out in the woods somewhere singing kumbaya."

"Fresh air is good, though. That boy already spends a lot of time on the computer."

She had a point, but I was sending him there partly because he loved computers and it was a skill he could use — especially living in Silicon Valley — but partly because I wasn't comfortable having him at the house while Michael and I were trying to figure things out. But I didn't tell my mom that since I didn't want her to worry.

Later, I met Taylor and Jessica for a late lunch at my favorite Mexican restaurant in town. We sat in a corner booth, the familiar sounds and smells of the restaurant around us, but I couldn't focus on any of it. My mind was elsewhere, trapped in a loop of fear and doubt. When I finally voiced my concerns to them, I could see the worry in their eyes.

"Jesus, Mel, this isn't a way to live your life," Jessica said.

I tried to keep the tears at bay. "The psychiatrist said these thoughts I'm having that won't go away are all from PTSD. He hoped that talking things over with Michael and spending time with him would help, but this horrible feeling that he's not really Michael just won't go away. Michael is upset that I can't seem to move on after everything we've gone through."

"It can't be that easy to just move on," Taylor said.

"Michael seems to have been able to do it. Why can't I?"

Taylor and Jessica both tried to reassure me that everyone handled things in their own way, so I shouldn't compare my recovery to Michael's. I knew that was true. My therapist said that too — but it didn't make things easier. I sighed and told them the rest of it.

"Dr. Kanzaria diagnosed me with complex post-traumatic stress disorder a few days ago."

"What is that, like PTSD on steroids?" Jessica asked, and despite the weight of the conversation, her comment made me smile. She always had a way of lightening the mood, even when things were dark.

"Sort of. It's a response to complex traumas, from repetitive exposure to traumatic events when my mind tells me there's little or no chance to escape. I spent almost three months with a psychopathic stalker thinking he was Michael. I was lying next to him in bed, thinking he was my husband. And then he tried to kill me. The man was the spitting image of Michael, so now every time I look at Michael, I'm seeing Irvin Skaggs. It triggers me and sends me down these paranoid dark places in my mind. It's a never-ending loop because they looked the same."

"That's horrible," Taylor said softly, reaching across the table to place her hand over mine.

"But it is Michael, Mel. You touched the scar," Jessica said, her eyes searching mine for any sign of doubt.

I nodded, but it was more out of habit than certainty. "Doctor Kanzaria says it's Michael. So do the SFPD detectives. And Michael is losing patience with me. It can't be easy dealing with my mental state. He went through a lot of trauma, worse than me. Getting chained up and all."

"You both went through something horrible, Mel. I

don't think one is worse than the other," Taylor said with empathy.

"Have you guys done it?" Jessica asked.

I looked at Jessica askew.

"What? It might help," she said.

"God, no. We haven't even kissed since I got out of the hospital. Everyone tells me that's my husband, but I feel like he's a stranger."

"You said it yourself, Mel. He's gone through a lot too, so maybe he's acting differently because he's also going through his own PTSD," Taylor said.

Dr. Kanzaria had said the same thing. But the change I felt seemed much deeper than that. Still, it was hard to explain it to them, so I sat quietly, stirring the straw in my watermelon agua fresca and watching the ice cubes clink against the glass. The truth was, I didn't know what to think anymore. I didn't know what was real and what was just a product of my damaged mind.

"What is it?" Taylor asked, her eyes narrowing as she watched me.

"You can tell us anything, Mel. It won't leave this table," Jessica added, growing serious now.

I looked up at them, tears welling up in my eyes. They were my best friends, the people I trusted most in the world, but even they couldn't understand the hell I was living in. Still, I needed to talk. I needed to say the words out loud, to make sense of the mess in my head.

"Seriously, Mel, we would help you bury a body if

you asked," Jessica said, trying to lighten the mood again, and this time we all burst out laughing. It felt good, even fleetingly, to have friends who had your back no matter what.

After the laughter died down, I took a deep breath and decided to unload on them.

"I met with Inspector Ganns, the lead detective on our case. He said the case was closed, but when I pressed him for definite proof that it was really Michael and not Irvin Skaggs — like DNA proof that would be irrefutable — he told me they were still waiting on the results, and it might take up to a year."

Jessica frowned. "I thought that DNA testing stuff was fast, like on *CSI* or *23andMe*. Send them your spit, and a week later, you get the results back."

"That's not how it works in the real law enforcement world," I said, shaking my head. "The lab is backed up with a long queue of DNA samples. Since our case is closed and Skaggs's death was ruled justifiable self-defense, it's low priority and at the bottom of the pile."

"So you have to live with this doubt in the back of your mind about Michael for maybe half a year or more," Taylor said, her voice tinged with disbelief.

"Exactly. I can't live like this for another day, let alone six months or a year. So Ganns gave me the number of his ex-partner, who retired from the SFPD and is now a private investigator."

Taylor and Jessica both leaned in closer. "No shit," Jessica said.

"I haven't even told my mom. It was before Michael and I talked, before he let me touch the scar. So I felt guilty about it afterward. I was going to call the PI the next day and cancel."

"Did you?" Jessica asked.

I shook my head, feeling the weight of my decision. "No. I figured if it could ease my concerns, it would be good for both of us. So what could it hurt? Because right now, I'm ready for a separation."

The words hung in the air between us, and for a moment, there was nothing but silence. Taylor and Jessica exchanged a glance, their faces strained with worry.

"Mel, are you sure about this?" Taylor asked, clearly concerned that I might be making a mistake.

I nodded, though I wasn't sure about anything anymore. "I don't know what else to do. I can't keep living like this, with this doubt eating away at me. I need to know the truth, one way or another."

"And if it's not Michael?" Jessica asked.

"It has to be him," Taylor said. "That Skaggs guy can't fool everyone twice. Come on."

I looked down at my hands, which were resting on the table. I didn't have an answer for that. I didn't know what I would do if the DNA results came back and confirmed my worst fears. But I couldn't let that stop me. I had to find out the truth, no matter how much it scared me.

"I guess I'll deal with that when the time comes," I said.

Taylor reached over and squeezed my hand, her touch warm and reassuring. "We're here for you, Mel. Whatever happens, you're not alone."

I was grateful for their support, but in truth I felt more alone than ever. The doubt, the fear, the uncertainty — it was all-consuming, and no matter how much I tried to push them away, they kept coming back, stronger and more terrifying each time.

THIRTY-FIVE
DEXTER

I SPEND MOST OF MY DAYS IN MY CAR, SO I FIGURED I would splurge and get a decked-out Audi Q8. Despite what the movies, TV and books said, being a PI wasn't chalk full of action. If you were good, it was actually quite dull, since no one would even know you were there. So I spent most of my time parked in my car at various nondescript locations around the Bay Area.

It was the reality of the private investigator business: endless hours of waiting, watching, and documenting the minutiae of other people's lives. One of the best skillsets of this job was having the patience of Job. I enjoyed slowly putting the pieces of a complex puzzle together. It also helped that the job paid well, and business had been very good.

It's why I'd splurged on the Audi after my last big case. A few years back, I wouldn't have dreamed of spending that kind of money on a vehicle, but the truth was, I spent so much time in my car that it made sense to invest in something comfortable, something that wouldn't leave me with a stiff back and sore legs after a twelve-hour stakeout. And let's face it — the PI business in San Francisco had been booming. Living alongside the tech moguls with too much money and not enough sense, I was busier than I'd ever been since putting up my shingle after retiring from the SFPD. I liked staying busy. I was only fifty-seven. Had been divorced for ten years. My kids were grown adults with families of their own. And I couldn't spend all day playing golf. So I might as well work and make more money in the next few years than I'd made as a cop.

The Reed case was different, which made it more exciting. It wasn't the usual infidelity, run-of-the-mill background check, or corporate espionage gig.

Melody Reed had come to me with a story that, frankly, I didn't quite know how to process at first. Her husband had built his writing career on elaborate stories with twisting suspenseful narratives. Melody's story — about the man she thought was her husband possibly being an imposter — was something straight out of one of those novels.

It sounded far-fetched, like something cooked up in a writer's fevered imagination. But the look in Melody's eyes when she told me about it was all too real. And I had followed the case of Irvin Skaggs, the obsessed fan who took over Michael Reed's life for three months, killing Reed's agent and almost killing him and his wife. No one disputed that. I followed up with Ganns, who confirmed it all to me. He also made it clear that as far he was concerned Irvin Skaggs was dead. And that hopefully I could help Melody find the closure she desperately needed to get on with life. So I was doing just that. It shouldn't prove too difficult to get the proof she wanted.

I'd been tailing Michael Reed for a week now, trying to gather anything that might help confirm or debunk Melody's fears. Now I needed to look around their home. The problem was, Reed didn't make it easy. He hardly ever left the house. His Pacific Heights mansion was like a fortress — high walls, security cameras, and a gate that could withstand a battering ram. Melody had given me the access codes to get inside, but Reed hadn't given me a window of opportunity to do that.

I'd been parked a block away from the house all morning, the gray skies of San Francisco mirroring the monotony of my task. My eyes flicked from the house to the screen of my tablet, where a GPS tracker showed the location of Reed's BMW. Melody had done as I asked, managing to plant the tracker in the spare tire compartment of his car without him noticing — a small victory in this otherwise frustrating case.

I sipped my coffee, the lukewarm liquid doing little to perk me up, and leaned back in my seat, thinking about how much of this job was waiting. And then more waiting. I'd seen Reed come and go a few times, usually for short errands, nothing significant. But today I needed more. I needed to get inside that house and see what I could find.

I glanced at the tracker again. Reed's BMW was still at the house. No movement. I drummed my fingers on the steering wheel, trying to decide if today was the day I'd make my move.

And then, just as I was starting to give up hope for the day, I saw the gate to the driveway open. A sleek black BMW rolled out onto the street. I quickly grabbed my camera, snapping a few shots as Reed drove away. He turned the corner, and I watched the tracker, waiting for him to get far enough away before making my move.

I gave it five minutes — long enough for Reed to be out of sight but not long enough for me to lose my nerve. Then I started the Audi and drove up the street, parking as close as I could to the house.

Before exiting my SUV, I took a moment to scan the area. The neighborhood was quiet. Satisfied that no one was watching, I stepped out of the car. I acted as casually as I could. Like I belonged there. I punched in the access code Melody had given me, the gate clicking open with a soft beep. I casually made my way into the Reed's property. Up the foot pathway leading up to the front door that looked like it weighed a ton. I used the key Melody had provided to unlock the door and slipped inside, closing it quietly behind me.

I had permission from Melody, so I wasn't strictly breaking and entering, but it wouldn't be good if Michael or anyone else would catch me roaming inside. Melody had let me know the schedule of their house cleaner and gardener, and they weren't expected that day.

The house was massive up close — ornate woodwork, large floor-to-ceiling windows with breathtaking views of the bay. I should have learned how to write novels, I thought while looking around. The interior was just as luxurious as I'd expected — dark wood floors, high ceilings, and artwork that probably cost more than my car. But I wasn't here to admire the decor. I moved quickly, keeping my footsteps light as I made my way through the house. I went up the stairs to Reed's bedroom first. I couldn't help but whistle. The bathroom was always a goldmine for investigators.

After about ten minutes there, I headed back downstairs and on to the backyard toward Reed's writing office. The door was closed. I tried the knob; it wasn't locked, so I opened it and stepped inside. The room was exactly what I'd pictured — a sanctuary for a writer, with bookshelves lining the walls, a white large desk in the center, and black shades on the windows to not distract from the task at hand. I took out my phone and started snapping photos, documenting everything.

I made my way to his desk, where the computer sat — sleek, modern, probably one of the latest models. Reed wasn't one to skimp on his tools of the trade, it seemed. I pulled out a small jump drive from my pocket, a nondescript black stick that contained software designed to quickly and discreetly copy the contents of a hard drive. It wasn't something I used often; getting caught with something like this was a surefire way to end up in a lot of trouble — but sometimes, it was the only option.

I pressed the power button on the computer, and it came to life with a quiet hum, the screen flickering on and displaying the familiar logo of the operating system. My fingers moved quickly, bypassing the password screen thanks to a little trick I'd learned a few years back. It wasn't perfect, but it got me in — most of the time.

Once the desktop loaded, I inserted the jump drive into one of the USB ports on the side of the computer; the device lit up with a small green LED. I opened the file explorer and navigated to the drive, double-clicking on the program I'd installed. A small window popped up, asking if I wanted to begin the transfer. I clicked "Yes," and the software went to work, silently copying every file, every document, every scrap of data from the computer onto the jump drive.

While the files transferred, I kept my eyes and ears open, constantly scanning the room, the hallway, listening for any sign that Reed might be returning. Adrenaline coursed through my veins, making every noise seem louder, every shadow more threatening.

The progress bar on the screen slowly filled up,

each percentage point feeling like an eternity. I wiped the sweat from my brow and checked the time. Reed had only been gone for about twenty minutes. I had hoped for at least an hour, but given the way things were going, I couldn't count on that. The GPS tracker showed his BMW still on the move, but I knew it wouldn't be long before he headed back home. While I waited, I picked up a small black notebook that was on the desk, the kind used to jot down ideas on the go. I flipped it open and scanned the pages.

It was filled with notes, hastily scribbled ideas, thoughts, and fragments of what looked like a novel in progress. The handwriting was erratic and illegible. Except for one word that he had written over and over: *Believe*.

Finally, the progress bar reached 100% and the software notified me that the transfer was complete. I let out a breath I didn't realize I'd been holding and quickly ejected the jump drive, slipping it back into my pocket. I closed the program, wiped the computer's recent activity logs, and shut it down, leaving no trace of what I'd done.

I stood there for a moment, my eyes scanning the room one last time. Everything was in its place, everything looked untouched. Good. I couldn't afford for Reed to know I'd been here.

I moved to the bookshelves next, scanning the titles. Most were what you'd expect — classics, reference books, and a few obscure texts that probably held special meaning for Reed. I looked for the makeup kit wrapped in a towel that Melody had shown me in a picture, but it wasn't there.

I checked my watch — twenty minutes had passed. I needed to move quickly. I took one last look around the room.

I pulled out my phone and checked the GPS tracker. Reed's BMW was on the move, heading back toward the house. My pulse quickened as I realized I had less time than I'd thought. I snapped a few more photos then quickly exited the office, retracing my steps through the house.

I made it to the front door just as the tracker showed Reed only a few blocks away. I slipped outside, quietly locking the door behind me, and made my way back to the Audi. I sat there, my heart pounding, drinking from a bottle of water. I saw Reed's BMW turn the corner, heading back home. I watched him pull into his driveway as the gate opened, and he drove inside before the gate closed.

I started the car and drove away. I exhaled, the tension finally leaving my body as I put some distance between myself and the house. I'd gathered some useful information, but it wasn't enough. Not yet. But it was a start. And in this business, sometimes a start was all you needed.

THIRTY-SIX
MELODY

Dexter texted me the password to Michael's computer late that evening. I stared at the message for a long time. The combination of numbers and letters on the screen seemed to blur together; my nerves made it difficult to focus. On the one hand, I was terrified of what I might find. There was also the feeling that I was betraying Michael's trust. The psychiatrist and the police had told me the case was closed; Skaggs was dead, and I had to move on. But I couldn't. And now this ultimate betrayal of hiring a private investigator to intrude into his life. If I was wrong about all this, he would never forgive me. How would I react if Michael did that to me?

I sat at the kitchen table, the house silent around me with those thoughts playing over and over in my mind. Michael had gone out for a late-night walk — something he had started doing recently, saying it helped him clear his head. I wasn't sure if I believed him, but I didn't question it. His absence gave me the time I needed to see what was going on in that studio.

Despite my guilt and misgiving about what I was doing, I took a deep breath, steeling myself, and I walked outside towards his writing studio. The door creaked as I pushed it open. It was dark inside. I hesitated at the threshold for a moment, but I went in.

I slowly approached the desk, my fingers trembling as I reached for the computer. The screen was dark, but a quick tap on the keyboard brought it to life, the familiar login screen appearing before me. I entered the password Dexter had sent me, my fingers moving with a mixture of determination and fear. The computer accepted the password, and the desktop loaded, revealing the usual assortment of icons and files. I wasn't even sure what I was looking for. I scanned the screen, my eyes landing on a folder labeled WIP. The book he had been working on all this time. I clicked on the folder. Inside was a Word document labeled "Untitled Manuscript." I clicked on it. My breath caught in my throat, a mixture of relief and anxiety swirling inside me for this betrayal of trust against Michael, but I continued perpetrating it.

I double-clicked the manuscript file. The document opened. "Untitled" was bold at the top of the page, and below it, neatly formatted in the manuscript style expected by the publisher, was the heading "Chapter One."

But when I scrolled down to the next page, my heart skipped a beat. The page was blank.

Confused, I scrolled further. "Chapter Two" appeared at the top of the next page, perfectly centered, but again, the rest of the page was empty. I frowned, my fingers trembling as I continued to scroll through the document. Chapter after chapter, page after page — it was all the same. Each chapter heading was there, neatly formatted and numbered in sequence, but every single page was blank.

"What the hell...?" I whispered in the stillness of the room.

I kept scrolling, faster now. Fifty chapters, three hundred and sixty-seven pages — every single one of them completely blank, except for the chapter headings. It didn't make any sense. Why would Michael go through the trouble of formatting an entire manuscript, only to leave it completely empty? What was he doing here every day, hours at a time for more than five months now?

I sat back in the chair, my breath coming in short, shallow gasps. The room seemed to close in around me. I had hoped that to see Michael's prose, his words that I knew so well, would make me certain it was him, offering me some kind of resolution. But instead, seeing those blank pages had only deepened the mystery, leaving me more confused and frightened than ever.

I closed my eyes, trying to calm the rising tide of panic within me. I had to stay focused. I had to figure this out. There had to be an explanation, something I was missing. Maybe the document was just a placeholder, something Michael had started but never finished. Maybe he had written the manuscript somewhere else, in another file, or maybe he had already printed it out and stored it away.

But much as I tried to rationalize it, the nagging feeling in the back of my mind wouldn't go away. This wasn't normal. This wasn't how Michael worked. He was meticulous, methodical — he didn't leave things unfinished, especially not something as important as a manuscript.

I opened the search function on the computer, typing in keywords, trying to find any other files that might be related. But there was nothing. Just the empty manuscript, staring back at me like a black hole, ready to swallow me whole.

I didn't know how long I sat there, staring at the screen, my mind a jumble of fear and confusion. Eventually, I forced myself to close the document and shut down the computer. There was nothing more to find here, nothing more I could do tonight. But the questions wouldn't stop swirling in my mind, each one more terrifying than the last.

As I stood up to leave, I glanced around the room, half expecting to find Michael standing in the doorway, watching me with that inscrutable expression I had come to dread. But the room was empty, silent except for the soft hum of the computer as it powered down.

I left the office, closing the door quietly behind me, and made my way back to the house.

In the kitchen, with hands that were still shaking, I poured myself a glass of water, trying to steady my nerves. I had to stay calm and had to keep it together. There had to be an explanation, a reason for all of this. I just needed to keep it together.

THIRTY-SEVEN
MELODY

I tossed and turned all night. Michael had spent the night in his writing studio. I wondered what he was doing there? Creating new empty chapters?

I got an email from Dash. Seemed like he was enjoying coder camp. I missed him terribly but was glad he was fifty miles south while Michael and I figured things out.

I was in the kitchen, cleaning up after breakfast when the intercom from the front gate buzzed. I glanced at the video monitor on the counter and saw an unfamiliar black sedan there. I wiped my hands on a dish towel, suddenly feeling nervous for some reason. I hit the intercom button asking who the visitors were. A brown-haired man in his thirties leaned out the driver-side window. He held out a badge to the video camera.

"Special Agent Edwin Torres with the FBI. Here to see Melody and Michael Reed."

I felt my heart beating faster. The FBI? What could they be here for, I wondered. "Come on in," I said as I clicked on the button to open the front gate.

I met them at the front door as the SUV parked. Two men exited the vehicle. "Mrs. Reed?" the man from the video, Edwin Torres said with a thin smile.

"That's right. What's going on? Everything okay?"

"May we come in?" Torres asked politely.

"Sure," I said, stepping aside to let them in.

I looked at the other agent, a man in his forties with thinning black hair. He held up his badge. "I'm Special Agent Jason Petrie. We work out of the San Francisco office."

It was surreal. I'd never met an FBI agent before, and to have two show up unannounced was a bit nerve wracking. The first thing that came out of my mouth was an offer of something to drink. Not sure why I did that. I get over polite when I'm nervous. Both men declined. I showed them to the living room, where we sat down.

I thought maybe they wanted to talk about what had happened to us since it was such a bizarre crime. Or did they have information that would set my mind at ease? Maybe they had the DNA results that proved it was Michael that had emerged from the bunker, victorious over Irvin Skaggs.

"Is this about what happened to my husband and me?" I asked.

Torres looked around. "Is Mr. Reed home?" he asked.

"Yes, he's in his writing studio. It's in the detached cottage in the backyard. I'll go get him," I replied, already moving down the hallway.

I knocked on Michael's office door and poked my head inside. He was sitting at his desk. He appeared to just be sitting there doing nothing.

"What is it?" he said, sounding annoyed that I'd interrupted his work.

"There are two FBI agents here to see us," I said, my voice trembling slightly.

That got a rise out of Michael. He looked at me, surprised. "The FBI? Really?" he said standing up. "Did they have a warrant?"

I wasn't expecting that from him. "I don't know. They wanted to talk to us, so I let them inside."

Michael sighed. "Never just let law enforcement into our home without a warrant," he said.

"Why?"

"Doesn't matter now, they're up in the house, right?"

I nodded.

"All right, let's see what they want," Michael said, making his way outside.

We walked back to the house in silence and joined the two agents in the living room.

"Mr. Reed, thank you for taking the time to speak

with us," Agent Torres said as Michael approached. Both agents then introduced themselves to Michael.

"What's this about?" Michael said curtly.

Agent Torres took a deep breath, his expression serious. "We received an anonymous tip that a private investigator, Dexter Mills, conducted unauthorized computer forensics on your personal computer."

I felt the blood drain from my face. I glanced at Michael, who looked at me with a mixture of confusion and anger. It hadn't even crossed my mind their visit could be about Mills.

"A private investigator? Who the hell is Dexter Mills?" Michael asked, sounding confused. Both agents looked at me.

My mouth went dry, and I struggled to find the words. "He's... he's the private investigator I hired," I admitted.

Michael's eyes widened in disbelief. "You hired a PI to investigate me?"

Agent Torres held up a hand, trying to keep the situation under control. "Mrs. Reed, while it's legal for you to hire a private investigator to conduct forensics on your own devices, Mr. Reed's computer is another matter entirely. Without his explicit consent. Even if you're married. Did you ask Mr. Mills to hack your husband's computer?" Torres said.

"Hack? What the fuck, Melody?" Michael said, looking at me with disdain.

"Mr. Mills's actions are a violation of federal law," the older agent, Petrie said.

Michael's face flushed with anger, his hands balling into fists at his sides. "You had someone break into my computer? Without telling me?" he practically shouted, anger at the betrayal evident.

"I didn't know he was going to do that!" I said. "I just wanted to make sure... I needed to know... after everything that happened, I had to be sure..."

"To be sure of what, Melody? That I'm not who I say I am? That I'm some kind of monster? I'm getting sick and tired of your bullshit," Michael said, his voice rising at each word he spoke.

Agent Torres stepped in once again, trying to diffuse the situation. "Mr. Reed, I understand this is a difficult time for both of you, but I need to make it clear that what Mr. Mills did was illegal. We have enough evidence to charge him with unauthorized access to a protected computer, and potentially other related charges. Are you interested in pressing charges?"

"What about her?" Michael asked.

I knew he was angry, but he wanted me arrested? I felt sick to my stomach; I could hardly breathe.

"That hasn't been determined yet," Torres said. It didn't exactly give me warm and fuzzy feelings.

Michael let out a bitter laugh, shaking his head in disbelief. "You've really outdone yourself this time, Melody. You didn't trust me, so you went behind my back and hired someone to invade my privacy. How could you?"

Tears welled up in my eyes, and I struggled to hold them back. "I'm sorry, Michael. I didn't know what else to do. After everything we've been through… I just couldn't shake the feeling that something was wrong. I didn't mean for it to go this far…"

Michael stared at me, his eyes cold and distant. The warmth, the love that had once been there was gone, replaced by something I never thought I would see from him: hatred.

Torres and Petrie asked more questions, but then I remembered what Michael had said about a warrant. And how he had lawyered up when the SFPD wanted to ask him questions about Irvin Skaggs. So I did the same thing. Michael seemed surprised I did that. Torres and Petrie looked at each other. Party was over.

"I'll be in touch, Mrs. Reed," Torres said. Both agents got up and began to leave.

On the way out, Agent Petrie said to Michael, "And Mr. Reed, I'm truly sorry for the intrusion. I hope you both can find a way to work through this." The agents left.

We stood in silence for about a minute.

"Wait here. I want to show you something," he said curtly as he headed up the stairs. He came back a minute later and handed me a piece of paper.

"What's this?" I asked.

"Look at it," he said.

I noticed the letterhead of the San Francisco Police Department. It was the DNA results. A surge of adrenaline hit me as I read the report, then it left me so suddenly I felt as if I would faint. There it was in black and white: the testing was complete and it confirmed that the DNA taken at the crime scene matched that of Irvin Skaggs. The report stated:

... thereby supporting the investigators' report that the perpetrator Irvin Skaggs was a victim of homicide by Mr. Michael Reed, which has been ruled as self-defense.

"When did you get this?" I asked.

"A few days ago," Michael said.

"And you're just showing this to me now?" I said, feeling angry.

"I didn't feel like I needed this report to prove who I am. And if my wife needed it, well, maybe we shouldn't be together anymore," Michael said.

My anger quickly morphed into guilt and shame. I had been so wrong, and put him through so much added trauma, after everything he had gone through.

He continued, "I was hoping you would come around without an official report, but instead you went out and hired a private investigator to spy on me."

I started to cry. "I'm so sorry, Michael."

"I can't do this anymore, Melody. I need you to leave."

His words hit me like a physical blow, and my knees buckled beneath me. "Michael, please, we can work this out. I'll do whatever it takes to make it right, I swear..."

But Michael shook his head, his expression resolute. "No, Melody. I need time to think. I can't be around you right now. Please leave. I'll call you in a couple days."

I packed a bag quickly, my movements mechanical. I couldn't focus on any one thought. With my bag in hand, I made my way to the door, pausing for a moment to look back at him. He still stood in the same spot, his back to me now. I wanted to say something, to reach out to him, but the words caught in my throat, and I knew it was too late.

I walked out of the house expecting him to stop me, but instead I heard the door closing behind me. It felt like the final nail in the coffin of our dying marriage.

I got into my car and drove away, tears streaming down my face as the city lights blurred around me.

THIRTY-EIGHT
MELODY

After Michael kicked me out of the house, I checked into the Four Seasons on Market Street. Michael called me and told me that for him to even consider taking me back, I needed to increase the frequency of my therapy with Dr. Kanzaria, which I agreed to do.

The therapy sessions were intense, and he had prescribed Zoloft for my PTSD and to help me with the feelings of depression at everything that had happened.

I checked out of the hotel after two weeks and drove down to San Jose to pick up Dash from coder camp. His excitement faded at not seeing his dad. I hated the hurt all this was causing my son. I had hoped that Michael would put aside the problems between us for the sake of Dash, but he wasn't ready. So I went down there by myself and told Dash that he would see his father in a few days — but for now, he would be staying with Grandma in Modesto.

"Are you guys getting a divorce?" he asked me matter-of-factly. Here I'd thought that despite everything I'd shielded him from our troubles, but I wasn't fooling him, only myself.

"We're working very hard to avoid that, honey; it's why you need to stay with Grandma for a few days while I go back down to the city, so Daddy and I can work things out."

Dash looked out the window of the car and didn't say anything.

"How does that make you feel, Dash?"

He seemed to think about it for a moment, then he turned back to me. "I don't want you guys to get divorced, so I feel happy you're trying to work things out. Don't worry, I'll give you guys space."

Although he was trying to be positive and supportive, those words pained me greatly. What I had put my son through because of my distrust and paranoia against his father...

The mood improved during the ninety-minute drive from San Jose to Modesto, thanks to a much needed pit stop along the way at the In-N-Out Burger in Pleasanton for Double-Double and strawberry shakes.

I stayed at my mom's for a couple nights. I planned to head back to the city, leaving Dash with Mom, while Michael and I decided what would be the next chapter in our lives. I hadn't seen him in the two weeks since he had asked me to move out. But now that I had been seeing Dr. Kanzaria frequently and was on medication, he was willing to talk.

The drive back to San Francisco felt like wading through a slog. The fog outside was thick, pressing against the car windows, but the real fog was in my head. Everything felt muted, like I was trapped behind a layer of thick glass. The medication had taken the edge off my fear, but it had left me numb, detached. My thoughts drifted, heavy and slow, as if I were watching someone else's life play out on a screen.

The moment I hit the Maze, the tangle of freeways leading up to the bridge, the traffic ground to a halt. Cars crawled forward in agonizing increments, hemmed in on all sides by a sea of brake lights. I gripped the steering wheel more tightly, my knuckles turning white. The stillness should have calmed me, but instead it heightened the sense of dread that I felt.

As I crossed the Bay Bridge, the city skyline emerged in front of me, but it felt more like a mirage than the city I had called home for more than ten years.

The world outside the car — buildings, lights, people — blurred past, surreal and unreachable, while my mind struggled to focus on anything but the growing pit in my stomach.

Doctor Kanzaria had warned me that the medication might take some time to adjust to, that the initial side effects could be unpleasant, but he'd assured me that it would help in the long run. I clung to that hope like a lifeline, even as the fog in my mind thickened. I wanted to get better, to be the wife and mother I used to be, the woman who could look at her husband without questioning if he was really who he claimed to be.

I turned onto our street. Pacific Heights was at the very top of a ridge that rose sharply from the Marina District and Cow Hollow neighborhoods 370 feet above sea level.

When I finally pulled into the driveway, my hands were trembling. I sat there for a moment, my sweaty palms gripping the steering wheel as I stared at the house. It was so quiet, so still, that it seemed almost abandoned. But I knew Michael was inside, waiting for me. I didn't know what I would say to him, how I would face him after everything that had happened.

Taking a deep breath, I turned off the engine and got out of the car. The air was cool, a slight breeze rustling the leaves of the trees lining the driveway. I walked slowly up to the front door. My fingers fumbled with the key, and for a moment I was afraid I wouldn't be able to get it into the lock. But then the door clicked open, and I stepped inside.

The house was just as I had left it a couple weeks ago — neat, orderly, everything in its place. But there was a heaviness in the air, a tension that seemed to press down on me from all sides. I could feel it in the silence, in the way the shadows clung to the corners of the rooms, refusing to be banished by the dim light filtering through the windows.

"Melody?" Michael's voice came from the hallway, and I stiffened.

I turned to see him standing there, his expression a mixture of relief and concern. He looked tired, worn down, as if the weight of the past few weeks had taken its toll on him too. It was something Doctor Kanzaria kept reminding me about: how Michael was also a victim of Irvin Skaggs and dealing with his own PTSD. I had been so damned selfish.

"I'm back," I said, sounding distant even to my own ears.

He nodded, taking a step closer. It was an awkward reunion. We treated each other as strangers more than husband and wife. "How was your appointment?"

I swallowed hard, trying to clear my mind. "It was... good. Doctor Kanzaria thinks the medication will help. He explained a lot of things to me, about the CPTSD, about why I've been feeling the way I have."

Michael's expression softened, and he reached out to take my hand. His touch was warm, grounding me in the present moment, pulling me out of my prescribed stupor just enough for me to feel the weight of his emotions. "I'm glad you're getting the help you need, Melody. I know this has been hard on you... on both of us."

I nodded, tears welling up in my eyes. "I'm sorry, Michael. I'm so sorry for everything I put you through.

I just... I didn't know how to handle it. I was so scared, so confused..."

He squeezed my hand, his grip firm, reassuring. "I know. And I'm sorry too. I should have been more understanding. We've both been through hell, and we need to be there for each other if we're going to get through this."

For a moment, I allowed myself to believe that everything would be okay, that we could rebuild what had been shattered. But as I looked into Michael's eyes, I couldn't shake the lingering doubt that gnawed at the edges of my consciousness. The medication had dulled my fear but hadn't erased it. I still wondered, deep down, if I was seeing the real Michael or if I lived in a nightmare of my own creation.

"Why don't we sit down?" he suggested, leading me into the living room. "I made some tea."

I followed him, he held my hand, but it didn't feel natural. We sat down on the couch, the silence between us heavy with unspoken words. Michael handed me a cup of tea, and I held it between my hands, the warmth from the cup seeping into my skin, but doing little to thaw the cold knot of anxiety in my chest.

"I've been thinking a lot," Michael began hesitantly. "About everything that's happened. I want to work on us, Melody. I want to get back to where we were before all of this."

I nodded, though I wasn't sure if that was possible.

The memories of what we had been through, of Irvin Skaggs and the horrors he had brought into our lives, were still too fresh, too raw. But I wanted to try. I had to try.

"Me too," I whispered. "I want that too."

He gave a small, tentative smile that didn't quite reach his eyes. "Then let's take it one step at a time. We'll get through this, Melody. We'll find our way back to each other."

I wanted to believe him. I wanted to move forward. But I felt like I was drifting, caught between reality and the lingering shadows of my fears. The Zoloft had numbed the edges of my anxiety, but it hadn't erased the terrible memories, the images that haunted me every time I closed my eyes. When I told the doctor about that, he'd warned me that therapy and medication weren't going to magically erase all these awful thoughts and visions in my head. "We can manage it, but there is no cure."

"I've been thinking too," I said, my voice trembling slightly, "about what Doctor Kanzaria said. He explained why I've been feeling this way, why I've been so suspicious, so distrustful. He said it's normal, given what happened, but..."

"But what?" Michael asked, his eyes searching mine.

I took a deep breath, trying to steady myself. "But I'm scared, Michael. I'm scared that no matter how much therapy I go through, no matter how many pills I take, I'll never be able to trust you again. He looked just like you. I'm afraid I'll never be able to look at you and not see him."

His expression tightened, a flicker of pain crossing his features. "Melody, I'm not him. I'm not Skaggs. I'm your husband, and I love you. I would never hurt you."

"I know that. I know it here." I touched my temple, feeling the pressure build behind my eyes. "But in here"—I pressed my hand to my chest, over my heart—"I can't stop the fear. I can't stop the doubt. It's like it's been burned into me, and I don't know how to get rid of it."

He reached out, cupping my face in his hands. "It's only been two weeks since you started with the medication. We'll figure it out, Melody. We'll take it day by day, and we'll get through this together."

I nodded, though I wasn't sure I believed him.

"I just want us to be okay." I leaned into his touch, trying to draw strength from him.

"We will be," he murmured, his lips brushing against my forehead in a tender kiss. "We'll be okay, Melody. I promise."

I managed a smile. I couldn't wait until we sold this house and moved somewhere else, where the memories of Skaggs didn't hang thick around every nook and cranny.

THIRTY-NINE
MELODY

A FEW DAYS LATER, I WAS PUTTING AWAY groceries and feeling better. I wasn't all the way back, not by a long shot, but I was more like my old self. The familiar routine of everyday tasks — stocking the fridge, wiping down the counters, arranging the fruit in the bowl on the kitchen island — was oddly soothing, like I was reclaiming pieces of my life that had been shattered when Skaggs barreled into my life, wreaking deadly havoc. Each simple act grounded me, reminding me of that past life.

I wasn't sure if I should have attributed feeling better to the medication kicking into full gear or just to the passage of time also doing its healing thing. It wasn't that I felt entirely like myself — far from it — but there was a lightness in my chest that hadn't been there in weeks, a glimmer of hope that maybe, just maybe, I could find my way back to some semblance of normalcy.

I was also excited to drive up to Modesto in the morning to pick up Dash. The thought of seeing his face, hearing his laughter fill the house again, made my heart swell. That certainly had a lot to do with why I felt happier than I had in weeks. My sweet boy, who brought so much joy — his presence would help me hold on, remind me of what was worth fighting for.

Things were moving slowly between Michael and me, but they did seem to be heading in the right direction. We were taking it day by day, step by step, trying to rebuild the trust that had been so brutally torn apart.

We still lived more like roommates than husband and wife. We hadn't tried to get intimate. I wasn't pushing for sex, and neither was Michael. My medication had set my sex drive to sub-freezer mode; Dr. Kanzaria had warned me it was a possible side-effect.

Jessica had suggested that I jump Michael's bones and screw the awkwardness between us away once and for all.

"If it were only that simple, Jess," I had told her, forcing a laugh, though the thought made my stomach churn.

I was putting a carton of milk in the fridge when my phone rang. I looked at the screen and cringed. I didn't expect to see that number displayed ever again. I paused, holding the cold metal handle of the refrigerator door, my grip tightening as I stared at the screen.

My brain told me to let it go to voicemail, but I couldn't help but to be curious why Dexter Mills was calling me.

I leaned against the refrigerator door, the cool metal pressing into my back as I stared at the phone in my hand, Dexter's name flashing on the screen.

My mind raced, torn between answering and letting it ring out. The investigation I'd hired him to conduct had blown up spectacularly after the FBI agents came to the house, reprimanding me for violating Michael's privacy. The memory of their stern faces, the veiled threats of legal action, and the look on Michael's face having found out what I had done, still made my stomach churn.

For weeks afterward, I'd been worried that I'd face real legal consequences—that I'd crossed some line I couldn't come back from. But in the end, my lawyer had calmed my fears, reassuring me that I was in the clear. I hadn't committed any crime. After all, it wasn't unheard of for spouses to hire private investigators to dig into each other's lives. I'd been driven by fear and desperation from everything Michael and I had been through. I wasn't thinking clearly—I was grasping for some semblance of control in a situation that had spiraled out of it. And Michael had understood that, or at least he'd pretended to. He'd refused to press charges, his cooperation with the authorities limited to a few curt responses, cutting the investigation short. The case had been closed just as quickly as it began, and I was left with the bitter aftertaste of relief, knowing I'd narrowly avoided disaster.

Still, that ordeal had left scars, ones I wasn't sure I'd ever fully shake. Now, standing in my kitchen, that familiar tension crept up my spine again as Dexter's call lingered.

I had paid Dexter in full, and I'd never thought I would hear from him again. That part of my life was over, as far as I was concerned. But my curiosity was piqued, so I answered the phone.

"Hello?" I said more quietly than I'd intended, almost as if I were afraid of what he might say.

"Mrs. Reed, it's Dexter Mills," he said, his tone carrying a layer of tension I assumed was due to him getting jammed up working on my case.

Although I had been left off the hook, I hadn't checked in on what price he might have paid for getting involved in my life. I felt guilty about that, which was one of the reasons I took his call.

"How bad did you get in trouble?" I asked him.

"Not too bad. Got lectured not to do anything like this again. I was more worried about the BCIS than the police, but since I wasn't charged and the case was closed, I got off with the warning."

The BCIS stood for the Bureau of Security and Investigative Services, which was the state agency in California responsible for licensing and regulating the alarm, locksmith, private investigator, private security, and repossession industries in the state. They held significant power over Dexter's career had they revoked his license to work as a private investigator.

"I'm glad to hear that," I said.

"How are you doing, Mrs. Reed?" he asked me with an earnestness that I wasn't expecting.

It caught me off guard, and I felt a lump form in my throat. He sounded genuinely concerned, like he cared, not just as a PI but as a person. I was starting to understand why Ganns had trusted him so much.

It took me a few seconds to regain my composure. "I'm doing better. I'm seeing a therapist. Taking some medication. I'm back home with my husband, and we're trying to work things out."

There was a pause on the other end, a pause that made my heart skip a beat. And then, finally, he said, "Oh. You're back at the house with him. Right now?" He said with an urgency that made me shiver.

"I am. Why are you asking me about that?"

"I know the case is over, but I have some information that you need to know about. Because if you're at home, I believe you're in grave danger."

My fingers tightened around the phone and I felt my pulse quicken.

"Danger? What are you talking about?" My voice sounded weaker than I intended, barely above a whisper.

"I've been doing some digging on my own," Dexter said, his tone steady but laced with urgency. "I couldn't let it go, Mrs. Reed. Something about the case—it didn't sit right with me. I've uncovered some things I think you need to hear."

I leaned forward, pressing the phone harder against my ear, my heart hammering in my chest. The kitchen suddenly felt too quiet, the silence between Dexter's words almost deafening. I glanced around, half-expecting Michael to appear behind me. But the house was still, eerily still.

"What things?" I asked, my throat dry. "You said I was in danger. What have you found?"

"Do you remember when you were in the hospital, recovering? Michael told you he had to fly down to LA to meet with some prospective new agents?"

I nodded, even though he couldn't see me. "Yes, I remember. I didn't think much of it at the time. I was so out of it, and he made it seem like it was something he had to do for his career after Lydia's death."

"Well," Dexter continued, "I tracked his movements during that trip. He didn't just go to LA, Melody. He went further south, down to Tijuana, Mexico."

I felt a cold shock of disbelief run through me. Tijuana? What the hell had Michael been doing in Tijuana? Aside from getaway trips to Cabo or the Riviera Maya, we had no ties to Tijuana and Michael didn't have any business dealings there. So why would he go there and hide that from me? My mind tried to piece together what Dexter was telling me.

"Why? Why would he go to Tijuana?" I asked.

"That's what I wanted to find out," Dexter said. "So I did some digging, and I found out he visited a plastic surgery clinic down there."

"Plastic surgery? What are you saying?"

"It's not just a run of the mill clinic down south where Americans get cheaper tummy-tucks. It's the kind of place that's known for doing anything you want, regardless of the risks or reasons. A place known not to ask questions and do whatever their patients want, as long as they have the money to pay for it."

I felt nauseous. Why would Michael go to a plastic surgeon in Tijuana?

FORTY
MELODY

I don't know how long I was silent, but next thing I remembered was Dexter asking me if I was okay.

"Plastic surgery?" I echoed, my voice weak. "Why would Michael need plastic surgery?"

"That's the $64,000 question, isn't it?" Dexter said grimly. "I couldn't get an answer on the phone or online, So I paid the clinic a visit. And after a little financial persuasion the clinic administrator was more than happy to share Michael's medical records with me."

My heart was pounding so hard I thought it might burst out of my chest. I could barely breathe, the fear and confusion choking me.

"What did they say?" I asked, barely able to get the words out.

"Michael was there for an outpatient procedure," Dexter said slowly, as if he were carefully choosing his words. "He brought them pictures of a scar — your husband's hernia scar. He wanted the doctors to replicate it on his own body, to make it look like he'd had the same surgery."

The room spun around me, and I had to grab the edge of the counter to steady myself. My thoughts swirled in a chaotic whirlpool of disbelief and horror.

"He... he had the scar made in Mexico?" I stammered, my mind struggling to comprehend what I was hearing. "Why would he do that?"

"Melody, listen to me," Dexter urged. "You weren't crazy before. You were right to be suspicious. Everything you felt, everything you feared — it's all real. This man, the man you're living with, isn't who he says he is. Your husband didn't kill Skaggs. I'm certain it's the other way around. That's still not Michael. He's the imposter. It's been him this whole time. Irvin Skaggs."

"No," I whispered, tears streaming down my face. "No, this can't be happening again. It can't be true. He showed me the DNA from the police. The dead man was Skaggs, not Michael."

"I checked on that with the SFPD and they still haven't tested it. It's a fake done on his computer to trick you."

My knees buckled, and I slid to the floor, the phone

clutched tightly in my hand. The world seemed to collapse around me, the truth crashing down with the weight of a thousand bricks. I felt like I couldn't breathe, a panic attack triggered by what Dexter had told me. I took deep breaths in an attempt to regain my composure.

But, deep down, I knew it was. I had known it all along, hadn't I? Every instinct, every doubt, every fear I'd had — this was the confirmation I had dreaded, the truth that had been staring me in the face all along, but everyone kept telling me it was in my head. What I knew deep down inside that that wasn't Michael had been watered down and mitigated with strong prescription drugs numbing into a comfort that put me and Dash in so much danger. I felt so stupid for letting this happen to me all over again. For not trusting in myself.

"I'm so sorry, Melody," Dexter said. "I didn't want to tell you this over the phone like this, but it's urgent that you knew about this right away, because you have to get out of there right away. You're not safe."

My hands trembled so badly I almost dropped the phone. I felt like I was trapped in a nightmare, one I couldn't wake up from.

"Melody, are you there? You need to leave," Dexter said.

"I'm here," I said feeling stunned.

"You need to leave right now. Don't let him know

you're onto him. Just get out, take Dash, and go somewhere safe immediately."

The thought of leaving, of confronting the man who had taken over my life, was almost too much to bear. But I knew Dexter was right. I had to protect myself and Dash. There was no other choice.

"I'll go," I said, my voice shaky but resolute. "Dash is at my mom's in Modesto, thank God, but I'll go there, right now."

"Good," Dexter said.

"I need to call the police," I blurted out, the words spilling out of me in a rush.

Dexter's tone changed, becoming more cautious. "I know you're scared, and you have every right to be. But calling the police right now might not be the best move."

"Why not?" I demanded. "Why shouldn't I call them? They can help, they can protect us."

"It's not that simple, Mrs. Reed. The police might not believe you. Right now, everything we have is circumstantial. There's no concrete proof that he's not Michael — at least not while there is a queue on the DNA. They might think you're just a paranoid wife, someone who's been through a traumatic experience and is seeing things that aren't there."

"But you've seen the medical records, Dexter," I insisted, clutching the phone like it was the only thing keeping me tethered to reality. "You saw the scar, the clinic in Tijuana. It's different than before — how can that not be enough?"

"I know, I know," Dexter replied. "But think about it from their perspective. The case is closed. The FBI is already involved because of my accessing Michael's computer without consent, and now I'm accessing his medical records after paying a bribe. We're on shaky ground."

I swallowed hard, the truth of his words sinking in. The thought of trying to explain everything to the police, of reliving all the trauma, all the doubts, felt like a mountain I wasn't sure I could climb. And what if Mills was right? What if they didn't believe me? Again. What if they thought I was just some crazed woman, still recovering from a CPTSD?

I agreed with him and ended the call. I sat there on the floor for what felt like an eternity, but it was just a few seconds, *get up*, I said to myself. I couldn't afford to fall apart now. I had to be strong, for Dash and for myself.

I stood up slowly, my legs shaky but determined. I had to get out of here before it was too late. How could I get out without alerting him? I pushed through the fear as I made my way out through the house. Every sound, every creak of the floorboards made me jump, my mind imagining the worst. I tried to be light on my feet but was terrified that I was making a racket that could be heard down the block. But I knew that was my head messing with me so I pushed forward, driven by the need to escape, to protect myself and Dash from the parasite that had attached itself to our lives, destroying it. I couldn't even take the time to process that if Skaggs was the one that emerged from the shelter alive, that meant my Michael was dead. But I couldn't think about that right now. Nor could I pack a bag. I just grabbed my car keys and my phone and I made my way towards the front door as quietly as possible.

I felt a sense of relief as I reached for the knob of the front door, I reached out for it with my hand, but I heard it click, and saw the knob turn. I took a step back, frozen as I heard the door creak open and he stood there blocking my exit.

"Where do you think you're going?" His voice echoed through the house, calm and steady. It's as of now I could see his true form. My Michael was gone. And I couldn't believe how I could have let this monster fool me. But there wasn't time to dwell on any of that. I had to run away.

I didn't say anything, I just turned back and took off running towards the sliding door that led out to the backyard, but I only made it a few feet when I felt his forearm around my neck like a hook pulling me back towards his chest. I screamed.

"You're not going anywhere," he hissed. I could feel his warm breath on the back of my head as his grip around my neck tightened then I felt a pin prick and he let me go. My hand went to my neck as I turned around and I saw him standing there looking at me with disdain. I turned to run again but felt my knees buckling as my vision blurred. I could feel myself stumbling, not running. What was happening to me? I thought as I fell to the floor. My reality seemed to melt away into a dark oblivion.

FORTY-ONE
MELODY

I PASSED OUT INTO DARKNESS, AND AWOKE IN IT AS well. But it was different as my eyes fluttered. My head throbbed, a dull, relentless ache that muddled my thoughts and left me swimming in a haze. Blinking the dark haze away didn't seem to help much. I felt like the world had tilted just out of reach, smearing my vision. My surroundings seemed vaguely familiar even though I had seemed to have lost my ability to focus my eyes.

Where was I?

I kept blinking, trying to get my vision readjusted, but my eyelids felt so heavy, making it hard to keep my eyes opened. I struggled with that for a while, until finally I managed to pry them open. But even doing that was a challenge. And it wasn't just my eyes — my entire body was sluggish, stuck in second gear. My entire body seemed to protest what I was trying to do and was uncooperative. I moved my arm to rub my temples and I heard the jangling of metal on concrete and I felt something tight around my wrist.

I yanked my arm to look at it, but it wouldn't move. Finally my eyes began to focus, and a sudden panic surged through me as I realized what was on my wrist holding me in place. It was a thick leather strap around my wrist with a chain attached to it. I followed it down to where it was padlocked into a steel hook anchored into the concrete floor.

The sudden horror felt like a physical blow, jolting me all the way out of my stupor. I tugged frantically, pulling my wrist in every direction, desperate to free myself. But the chain held firm, rattling with a mocking sound. I reached for my other wrist, only to find it shackled too. And my ankle — the cold bite of the restraint there made my stomach churn.

The room shifted in my vision, and the darkness didn't seem so absolute. A faint light, fluorescent and sickly, flickered at the edges of my sight, and I knew where I was.

I was back in the damned bunker. The old bomb shelter that Michael had been so excited to refurbish, and that was meant to protect us, had again been turned into a prison. First to hold Michael captive, now me.

I began to thrash like a wild animal caught in a trap pulling and yanking at my restraint.

My wrists throbbed where the metal dug into my skin, but I barely noticed the pain. Memories trickled back, slipping through the haze that had gripped my mind.

I had been in the kitchen, talking to Dexter Mills on the phone. He had uncovered the truth — the horrifying, sickening truth that it was Skaggs that had made it out of the bunker alive. Not my Michael. I was getting ready to leave the house, thinking Skaggs was in the writing studio, only to find him standing there in the foyer. I'd been too late to escape.

I remembered his voice behind me, and then in an instant his iron grip around my neck. I could feel his warm breath on my skin making me sick and then I felt the prick of a needle in my neck. I saw him standing there with a syringe in his hand as I began to pass out.

The warmth of whatever he had injected into me had coursed through my body, pulling me down into a fog that no amount of willpower could fight against. I remembered stumbling, grasping for something to steady myself. He'd watched me, seemingly amused, as I blacked out. His face was blurring and fading. And then... here I was. Chained up like an animal in the same shelter where Skaggs had tortured Michael, had taken his life — and now he had me trapped in here.

A wave of nausea rose in my throat, and I fought to keep it down. The truth of it all was suffocating. I felt trapped and helpless. My phone call with Dexter saying not to get the police involved. The horrible realization that no one was coming to rescue me. Michael was gone — Skaggs had killed him, stolen his life, and I was his next victim. Why else would he lock me up down here? Why was I still alive? I now understood why he had kept Michael alive to write the books he couldn't write. What could I offer him to keep me alive? Nothing.

Tears burned at the corners of my eyes as I realized that my dire situation seemed to be getting worse by the second but I clenched my teeth and swallowed them. Crying wouldn't save me. Nothing would save me now. But then a single thought pierced the overwhelming panic.

Dash.

A sob tore from my chest at the thought of my son growing up orphaned. And what if this sick fuck tried to hurt him? It was obvious Skaggs wanted nothing to do with Dash. My stomach twisted painfully. I had to get out of here. I had to protect Dash. How? I pulled at the chains again, harder this time, ignoring the bite of metal into my skin. But it was useless. The restraints were solid, inescapable.

I slumped back, panting, the cold concrete pressing against my spine. My mind raced, searching for any solution, any way out of this nightmare. I was still alive, so Skaggs wanted something from me. He wouldn't have gone to those lengths if he didn't. That gave me time — time to think, time to figure out how to escape. But how much time?

The fear gnawed at my mind, eroding my focus. I forced myself to breathe, trying to steady the horrific thoughts that crashed through my brain. I couldn't let the panic win.

The minutes stretched, turning into what felt like an eternity. My strength ebbed with the relentless fear and exhaustion from struggling against my restraints and whatever knockout drug he had injected into me. Just when I felt the last sliver of hope slipping away, a sound broke the oppressive silence. I heard the hatch door opening and then footsteps. He was coming down the ladder.

I froze, my pulse quickening. The heavy thud of each step echoed through the shelter, deliberate, slow. Then he was walking up towards me, nonchalantly.

"Melody. You're awake," he said, smooth and chilling.

Skaggs. Aside from utter fear, I also felt humiliated that twice he had fooled me. It was surreal, how he had completely impersonated Michael. Not just the physical appearance, but the way he talked and walked. Like Cordyceps attacking its host. Invading it, until it eventually replaced the host. It's what Skaggs had done. He was like a human fungus who had attacked Michael.

Icy terror washed over me, so intense it numbed my body. I knew then that my time was running out.

But I wouldn't let him break me. I wouldn't give him the satisfaction of seeing or feeling my fear.

I lifted my chin, summoning every ounce of strength I had left to face that son of a bitch.

If I couldn't save myself, I would make sure Dash never fell into his hands. Even if he killed me.

FORTY-TWO
IRVIN

I DIDN'T WANT IT TO GO DOWN THIS WAY, BUT SHE gave me no choice. I had ignored the Melody situation for way too long. My plan from the start was to divorce her and move far away from her, but it was too late for that, she had forced my hand. My mind buzzed with the clarity of purpose that had eluded me for so long. The frustration, the anger, all of it crystallized into a single, unwavering resolve. Melody had to die.

From day one, she had become a problem, a thorn in my side that needed to be plucked out, for good. No matter what I did she continued to me see with distrust in her eyes which is why I had avoided her. I could see her pick up small tells that I wasn't the Michael Reed she had married. I couldn't explain to her that I had taken my rightful place as the real Michael Reed. If I didn't have that damned book to write, I might have had more time to deal with this differently. I had been patient, more patient than anyone in my situation would have been with her accusatory eyes. But every man had his limits, and I had reached mine.

I couldn't just kill her though and make her disappear. After everything that had happened that would raise too many more red flags. There had to be another way to deal with this problem, permanently. The plan took shape in my mind, each step methodical and precise. If I was going to succeed in keeping the life that rightfully belonged to me, my plan had to be perfect. I couldn't afford long-simmering doubt about what happened or for the police to be suspicious about what was going to happen.

Unlike before, there must be no loose ends, no room for error. This was my chance to finally rid myself of the burdens of Michael Reed's past, to carve out the future that I deserved. The future that had been stolen from me by Michael Reed. He was gone, but Melody and Dash clung to the memory of him. And they have the audacity to look at me as if I'm the imposter. I could never move on as Michael Reed with them in the picture.

There was no way around it. Melody and Dash had to go. And she had been laying the groundwork beautifully for me all on her own.

The police already saw her as unstable, teetering on the edge of a mental breakdown. Diagnosed with CPTSD and on powerful antidepressants. It wouldn't take much to make the authorities believe her anguish had pushed her over the edge. The foundation was laid; all I had to do was set the final pieces in motion. A tragic tale of a woman whose battle with CPTSD was lost in the most horrible way imaginable. A mother, killing her own child, then taking her own life.

I couldn't move forward in my hard-fought life with that kid around. It had to be a clean break, and this was the perfect way to take out two birds with one stone.

The world would mourn for me, the beloved author that lost his family due to the mental illness of his wife.

It would be a neatly packaged explanation about what was about to happen here: murder-suicide. And I would be left alone, grief-stricken — in front of the authorities and the media, of course.

I glanced around the writing studio. This office, this house, was a prison. I needed to break free of them as well, to shed the skin of this life and emerge reborn on the other side.

The new Michael Reed would rise from the ashes of the old, unencumbered by the past, by the memories that had haunted me for so long. I'd move far away from here. Maybe out of the country for a few years. Somewhere nice, like Costa Rica. Or play it extra safe, perhaps a country without extradition to the US, like Indonesia or Vietnam. But I was getting way ahead of myself. I still had a lot to do before getting to that next stage of my life.

The thought of Dash sent a flicker of something deep inside me — was it guilt? Those were emotions I'd never had to contend with, so whatever I felt, I quickly squashed it. The kid was innocent, yes, but he also linked me to a life I needed to leave behind. Besides, he would be better off joining his mother and father in the afterlife. I was not one for kids. Sad, really, killing a child, but a necessary part of my plan.

I would make it quick for him, painless. It was the least I could do.

I already had Melody chained up in the bunker. The kid would be back here in the morning. I checked the time; I had less than twenty-four hours to set everything up perfectly. And it had to be perfect for me to walk away scot-free.

Melody's blood work would show that she had combined her prescribed antidepressant with ketamine. I'd already shot her up with plenty of ketamine, but I would give her another shot. Then I would make sure to push her alcohol level to intoxication. The picture of a tormented woman would emerge: depressed, in a mental health crisis, drunk and drugged up — it wouldn't be much of a leap for the authorities to conclude that she'd snapped, killed Dash, then herself. Leaving me to find their bodies.

I would need to prepare, to make sure every detail was accounted for. The medications were easy enough since she had a prescription; the ketamine I'd picked up in Tijuana, so it couldn't be tied back to me. And I had already planted the seeds of doubt in everyone's mind about Melody's state. She had been doing a bang-up job on that front all on her own.

But there were other things to consider: how to make it look natural, how to ensure no traces left behind could implicate me. I had studied enough true crime novels and documentaries to know the pitfalls, the mistakes that amateurs made. I wouldn't make those mistakes. I couldn't afford to.

The world would mourn her, but I would not. I would be free, free to live the life that I had fought so hard to reclaim.

I checked the time. It was almost midnight. The driver would be dropping off Dash at the house at around ten in the morning. That should give me enough time to put everything in place. Within twenty-four hours of his arrival, Dash and his mother would be dead.

FORTY-THREE
MELODY

The air in the shelter was thick with tension, the silence broken only by the faint, distant hum of the ventilation system. I had been working on one of the metal hoops in the floor to which one of my chains was hooked. I kept bending it back and forth hoping I could break it off. It was going slow, and the damned thing wasn't budging much. I would take a rest and look around. My blood raced as I listened for any sound from above, any hint that Skaggs was coming. I wasn't sure what he would do to me if he caught me trying to escape, but I knew my chances of getting out here alive were not good, regardless.

And then I heard it — the metallic sound of the hatch opening and then the sound of footsteps descending the ladder. A minute later there he was, standing in front of me, his silhouette stark against the dim light from the hallway leading to where I was chained up. He stood there in the dark for a moment, then he stepped forward past the overhead fluorescent light and I could see his face and eyes locking on mine.

"You've caused me a lot of trouble, you know that?"

I couldn't believe he had the gall to say that to me. The parasite that had taken over Michael's life and infected and festered my entire world with his delusions and disease. But I swallowed hard. I had to keep it together for Dash who would be home soon.

"Please," I begged. "You can do whatever you want to me, but leave Dash out of this. He's just a child. Please."

Skaggs shook his head slowly, a sad smile playing on his lips. "It's not that simple, Melody. I wish it were. But you and Dash... you'll be together soon, at peace for eternity. That's the only way this can end."

A wave of panic crashed over me. I couldn't let this happen. I couldn't let him kill my son. "No!" I screamed. He was standing right in front of me, so I lunged at him, my hands reaching for his eyes, but the restraints held me back.

In one swift movement, he grabbed my wrists, twisting them behind my back and he shoved me to the ground. I struggled against him, kicking and thrashing, but he was too strong, his grip on me felt like iron.

"Stop fighting, Melody," he hissed, pulling a syringe from his pocket. "It'll be over soon."

FORTY-FOUR
MELODY

I woke up to the sensation of my body sinking into the soft mattress beneath me. This wasn't the cot in the bunker. The familiar scent of our bedroom filled my nostrils — the faint perfume of lavender from the sheets, the subtle musk of Michael's cologne lingered in the air. I opened my eyes and recognised our bedroom. It had all been a horrible nightmare. But something was wrong — terribly wrong. I couldn't move my limbs; it felt as if a heavy weight had crushed me and made me immobile. I tried to get up, but my body refused to obey. I tried to lift my arm, even wiggle a finger, but nothing happened. I couldn't even summon the strength to speak. It's as if my mouth had been glued shut. The only part of my body that I could still control were my eyes.

The curtains were drawn and the room dimly lit, but I could tell it was daylight outside. I had put a lot of care into finding the perfect curtains to block out the sun that yet looked stylish. Now they seemed to be Skaggs's accomplices in whatever he was planning to do because for whatever reason, I was still alive. Our entire lives, our home, and everything in it, seemed to have turned to black. Poisoned by Skaggs's evil.

I tried to turn my head, to see what was going on, but even that was a monumental task. My neck barely responded, offering only a slight tilt. And that's when I saw him.

Skaggs sat in a chair beside the bed, his posture unnervingly relaxed, as if he had been sitting there for hours, watching me. Waiting for me to wake up.

A smile curled the corners of his lips as he caught my feeble attempts to move. I couldn't feel any restraints on me so why couldn't I move?

I no longer felt fear in his presence. I felt rage and hatred for this sub-human thing that wanted to be Michael. He might have accomplished a physical metamorphosis with surgeries and his years spent working at being Michael, but his insides were too rotten to transform fully into Michael Reed. Irvin Skaggs would always emerge from the dark recesses, no matter how hard he tried. He would always be the imposter. I wanted him to know that, but I couldn't say the words.

"Oh, good, you're up," he said with casual cruelty, as if he were bringing me breakfast in bed. He leaned forward, elbows on his knees, looking more like someone about to share a fun secret than a killer with a sinister plan. "Don't bother trying to move or speak, Melody. I gave you and Dash a little something to keep you both still. The right dosage brings on a temporary paralysis. The type of anesthetics used for surgery. On the street they call it the zombie drug. Fitting, isn't it?"

I felt my heart pound wildly in my chest, and my eyes, darting around the room after he had said that he had given this same drug to Dash. I wanted to scream, to thrash, but my body betrayed me, bound in this eerie, motionless state. The most dread I had felt in all this was when the monster said my son's name. I wanted to yell at him to not speak his name. What had he done to Dash?

"It's okay, Melody. Dash is right next to you," he said.

I moved my eyes as far as I could to my left. In my peripheral vision I could see the shape of a small boy laying next to me. My eyes darted widely up and down and I saw his face with his eyes closed. It was Dash. He was lying still next to me.

I could see his chest rising and falling with shallow, rhythmic breaths, thank God, he was alive. His face, serene in sleep, shattered what little resolve I had left to fight this son of a bitch. Seeing my beautiful boy, unconscious and defenseless, broke me all the way down. I wanted to reach out and hug him, to comfort him, tell him everything was going to be alright. But I couldn't move an inch. I felt a surge of anger and an adrenaline rush. The protective mother in me wanted to jump out of this bed and lunge at Skaggs. I wanted to pummel him. Kill the bastard for what he had done to my family with my bare hands, but I couldn't do anything but lie there helpless and hopeless as tears rolled down my frozen face.

Skaggs followed my gaze and chuckled darkly. "Don't worry, Melody. He's fine, just sleeping. But you? You needed to be awake for this. The police wouldn't buy it otherwise. That's why I brought you back to the house and I've been waiting for you to wake up." His voice dropped to a conspiratorial whisper. "You see, a mother has to be conscious when she takes her son's life and then her own."

I wanted to recoil, scream, anything, but all I could do was blink away tears as his words felt like a knife to my heart. My throat tightened as panic surged higher; it felt as if the despair was drowning me. If he was going to hurt Dash, I wanted him to kill me first. Skaggs reached into his jacket pocket and pulled out a crumpled piece of paper, holding it in front of my face with a wicked gleam in his eyes.

"Your suicide note," he said with sickening pride. "You know, I've been struggling with writer's block for so long, staring at blank pages, but this..." He waved the paper tauntingly. "This flowed so easily. My best piece of fiction yet, I would say. Worthy of the great novelist, Michael Reed."

He read aloud, seemingly wanting to torture me with words. The note detailed a mother's despair, how grief had driven me to madness, to take the life of my only child and then my own. I felt bile rise in my throat. I could exit this world, I was ready, but not my Dash. And the thought that the press would report that I had killed my son was more of a torture than if Skaggs began pulling out my fingernails with rusty pliers. The words twisted and turned in my mind, barely registering as the edges of my vision darkened. I could feel myself slipping — slipping away into the void of paralysis and terror. But I fought with every ounce of my will to stay conscious. I couldn't lose myself now. Not now. I couldn't give up on Dash.

Skaggs finished reading the cursed note and placed it on the edge of the bed. He then pulled a knife. I recognized one of my kitchen knives. This couldn't be happening.

He wore black gloves. I saw him grab my right hand and he forced it to grip the handle of the knife. With his left hand he propped me up and I could see Dash laying there. I felt like a rag doll in his hands. He used my hand to guide the knife up over Dash's chest. He reared the knife back into a stabbing position readying to plunge it into his body and there was nothing I could do but watch him use my hand to kill my son.

Suddenly, a loud crash echoed through the room. My senses snapped into sharp focus. I was able to slightly crane my neck toward the sound of the noise. It seemed the drug was beginning to slowly dissipate. I couldn't tell what was going on, but Skaggs let go of me and my listless body fell back onto the bed. I heard Skaggs yell.

"What the fuck?" I couldn't tell what was going on but felt him jumping out of the bed.

I heard another voice yell: "Don't move you piece of shit!"

It was Dexter Mills.

"Drop the fucking knife, Skaggs!" Dexter's voice was a bark, strong and commanding, cutting through the thick tension like a blade.

I heard Skaggs voice. "All right, all right," he drawled, his voice deceptively calm.

I could now move my wrist and wiggle my toes. And I was able to crane my head even further and I could see the back of Skaggs as he bent down and I heard a clunk on the floor.

"Goood, now kick the knife towards me," Mills said.

"You got it. No need to shoot, Mister PI man. I'll go quietly. Shit, I never thought I would get this far," he added, looking back at me with a smirk as he winked at me.

For the first time, I could detect a bit of Kentucky mountain man twang as he spoke. It seemed when his back was against the wall, he would reveal more of his true self. Or perhaps he knew it was all over, so he dropped the act. But deep inside, I knew he wouldn't go down easily without putting up a fight.

Skaggs turned back to face Dexter. His back faced me, and I saw him slowly reaching for a gun he had tucked in his pants at the small of his back. I yelled out to warn Dexter, but the words came out slurred and mumbled.

My body screamed in silence. I could now wiggle my entire legs, which I did frantically, trying to warn Dexter about the gun. It all happened in a second. Dexter's eyes darted in my direction at that same moment as Skaggs made his move. I couldn't believe how fast Skaggs pulled out that gun and raised it in Dexter's direction as the PI's eyes returned to Skaggs.

The sound of gunshots cracked through the air. It was so loud it made my ears ring. I watched, helpless, as Dexter staggered back. He yelped and clutched his shoulder. My heart seized in my chest. I couldn't see what was going on clearly, but it looked like Skaggs had shot him. No, no, no.

Dexter fell to the ground and I heard three more gunshots and I could see Skaggs body jerk backward as his shoulders caved forward. Skaggs recoiled back, making a half turn towards me in the bed. I could see him stagger closer towards me, his eyes widened in shock, blood spewed from his mouth. He raised his gun at me and I heard another gunshot and saw a red mist in the air then I felt it's warm splattering on my face and what looked like a wig coming off his head, but it wasn't a wig it was part of his skull blown up as Skaggs crumbled to the floor.

The immediate silence that followed strangely seemed as loud as the gunshots. The air was thick with the scent of gunpowder and the echo of violence that had just gone down in my bedroom. I had regained more of my movement and could prop myself up halfway in bed, leaning on my elbows, my upper body slightly raised. I looked down on the floor and stared at Skaggs's lifeless body lying there like a tribute at my feet. A copious amount of blood drained from the hole in his head. I then heard Dash moaning as the drugs began to wear off him too.

I still couldn't see Dexter. Was he dead too? Finally I could speak even though my words were slurred.

"Dexter? Are you okay?"

"Bastard got me once, but I'm okay," he said. His voice sounded like music to my ears.

I saw Dexter slowly walk up towards Skaggs's body, the gun trained on him. He looked down at the body as he holstered his gun. "He's dead," he said.

It was a surreal moment. Before all this, I always had said that no matter what a person had done, they deserved compassion, and no one deserved to be killed violently. But that was when I had the luxury of watching someone else's horror on television from my multi-million-dollar home. Now that I had lived through a horror of my own, all I felt was joy that Skaggs was dead. If my body were totally recovered, I might have even reached for Dexter's gun and shot him a few times myself.

Reality returned to me from that dark fantasy when I saw Dexter was bleeding.

"Dexter. Are you okay?" I said.

"I'm fine. He just grazed my arm. Bastard was a quick draw. I'll give him that," Mills said.

"Not fast enough, thank God," I said with a smile.

"Mom," Dash said, his voice groggy and hoarse.

I was now able to sit up but felt light headed. I was so overcome with joy that the nightmare was over.

"I'm here, honey. Everything is going to be okay."

Dexter went to the bathroom. I heard him turning on the faucet sink. I assumed he was taking care of his wound, but he came out with a wet towel and handed it to me. He pointed at his face. I looked in the mirror and realized to my horror that I was covered in Skaggs's blood. I looked like Carrie at the prom. I quickly turned away from Dash. I didn't want him to regain his consciousness and see me like this.

"Thank you," I told Dexter as wiped the blood away. "For everything," I said.

He smiled at me as I heard the sounds of sirens coming closer. I wanted to hug Dash, but the effects of whatever drugs Skaggs had given me were still causing havoc in me as I collapsed back down on the bed. I felt like I was on an out of control Tilt-A-Whirl ride as I faded away back into the void.

FORTY-FIVE
MELODY

When I woke up again, I was in a hospital room. *Not again*, I thought as I looked around at the bright sterile lights and sounds of the hospital. I could see an IV hooked up to my arm. My body ached, but the paralysis was gone, replaced by a dull, throbbing pain that radiated through my limbs.

My first thought was of Dash. Panic surged through me as I remembered the bedroom, remembered Skaggs and the horror of what he had tried to do. Dexter bursting through the door and a shootout in my bedroom. Did that really happen?

"Dash," I blurted out as I struggled to sit up, but a gentle hand on my shoulder stopped me from getting up.

"Take it slow, Melody," I looked up and there was a kind woman in scrubs looking down on me. I looked back at her with what must have been a confused look.

"I'm Dr. Sara Fiedler. You're at the San Francisco General Hospital. We're flushing out the drugs from your system while hydrating you," she said.

"It's okay, honey," a voice I recognized instantly said softly, and I turned to see my mother standing beside the bed, her eyes red-rimmed.

"Dash is fine. He's safe," she said with a warm comforting smile.

I sagged back against the pillows, relief washing over me in a wave. "Where is he?" I croaked.

"He's with Taylor and Jessica," my mom said, brushing a strand of hair from my forehead. "He doesn't remember anything, honey. He thinks he just came home and fell asleep. He's going to be okay."

"How long have I been here?"

"Just a few hours. Both you and your son can go home tomorrow. We just want to keep you overnight to be extra cautious," Dr. Fiedler said.

Tears filled my eyes this time they were tears of joy.

"It's over, honey. Irvin Skaggs is gone. For sure this time," my mom said.

"Thank God," I whispered.

THE NEXT DAY, I still felt a little lightheaded, yet regaining control of my body made me feel like Superman. I packed, eager to leave the hospital. But before I left, I took the elevator up to the sixth floor where Dexter was recovering from his gunshot wound.

I had found out that it was more serious than the graze he had told me back at the house, but they were able to remove the bullet and he would be going home in a few days and would make a full recovery.

He was propped up in bed flipping through an iPad when he looked up at me as I entered his room. He smiled when he saw me.

"How's Dash?" he asked right away.

"He's doing pretty good, all things considered. Thanks to you," I said, sitting down in the chair beside his bed.

He waved me off as if I were embarrassing him.

"I'm glad you're both okay."

"I don't know how to explain any of this to him, and that his father isn't coming back."

"I'm really sorry, Melody. I can't imagine what you're going through. I will say that unfortunately I've seen kids put through the ringer countless times during my law enforcement career — and they bounce back pretty well with proper care. For adults, it's more complicated. So make sure to take time for yourself to heal as well, Melody."

I smiled. I knew what he was saying. I had yet to really process any of what had happened.

"How did you know to come to the house?"

Dexter shrugged. "I've been doing this for a long time. I had a bad feeling after we talked. So I tried to check on you, but when I couldn't reach you, I knew something was wrong. That tracker was still in the car so I knew Skaggs was at the house. I pinged your phone, but it was offline. I knew there was no way you would shut off your phone, so I headed over to your place. I saw your car so I knew you hadn't been able to leave as you had planned. I still had the access codes, so I used them to get inside quietly since I didn't want Skaggs to know I was there and I walked into that horror show. I'm just glad I got there in the nick of time."

"Me too," I whispered, my voice thick with emotion. "Thank you, Dexter. For everything." I gave him a hug.

"You're welcome," he said, hugging me back.

FORTY-SIX
MELODY

In the month since leaving the hospital, I had only been back to the house a handful of times to pack up my things. I felt the place was cursed and chock full of horrible memories.

I split my time between Modesto and a house I rented in Mill Valley. I finally had mustered the courage to put this chapter of my life in the rear view mirror. So I returned to our stately home in Pacific Heights for the last time.

The house was a hive of activity. Movers were packing up boxes, loading furniture onto trucks. My mom, Taylor, and Jessica were there, helping with the last of the packing. The real estate broker hovered nearby, practically salivating over the new listing. I was eager to be rid of it. Too many bad memories there now.

I stood in the middle of the chaos, feeling strangely

detached from it all. It's as if Skaggs had erased the good memories I had living here before he showed up. This house and this life we had here were tainted now, stained by the horrors that had unfolded within these walls. I knew I could never live here again, never look at this place without remembering what had happened.

I wandered into Michael's writing studio, the room where he had spent so many hours crafting his novels, the place where the doppelgänger had tried and failed to continue his stolen legacy. The air felt heavy, a blend of memories and loss. I planned to donate Michael's writing computer to his alma mater, but today, I just needed to be here, to confront the space that had once been his sanctuary.

His desk and chair were still in their usual spots, but I had packed away the trophies, awards, and framed book cover posters. Someday, I would proudly display them again, but not today. Today, the weight of what was lost was still too raw, too fresh. Yet, I took comfort knowing that Michael's books would continue to bring joy to readers long after I was gone. And Dash —he had started writing short stories. Perhaps one day, he would follow in his father's footsteps.

My fingers grazed the edge of Michael's desk, and I remembered that strange moment when I had discovered the imposter's so-called manuscript—perfectly formatted, but devoid of any words. The irony wasn't lost on me. The doppelgänger had stolen Michael's life, but he could never steal his talent, his creativity. He was nothing more than an empty shell, just like those blank pages he had left behind.

I stood there for a moment, letting that sink in. It had taken me far too long to realize that I had been living with an imposter, but as everyone kept telling me, it wasn't my fault. "He had us all fooled," my mom had said more times than I could count.

I thought back to my recent lunch with Dexter at Zuni Café. His words had stuck with me, offering a kind of solace I hadn't found elsewhere.

"You have to stop beating yourself up about that," he had told me, leaning in with an intensity that belied his usually calm demeanor. "Skaggs had been planning this for decades. It's all he did when he was in prison—planning how to become Michael Reed. He had the time, the resources, and the obsession. A quarter of a million dollars in plastic surgery alone to perfect his disguise."

"I still should have known," I replied, feeling the weight of my guilt pressing down.

"You *did* know, deep down. But he manipulated you. That's what people like him do. He was smart enough to keep his distance, hiding out in that cottage to avoid you piecing it together. He knew you were growing suspicious."

Dexter took a long sip of his espresso, then met my eyes. "And remember—Skaggs fooled the SFPD too.

He was a master manipulator. It's going to be a case studied for years in psychology classes."

I had smiled at that, though it felt bittersweet. "I just wish the world would stop obsessing over it. I've been warned there will be podcasts, a Netflix documentary, maybe even a movie. I want to move on, but it's like I'll have to relive it over and over."

Dexter had placed a hand on mine, offering a small, genuine smile. "It's your story, Melody. But how you move forward with it, that's *your* choice."

I shook off the memory, blinking back the tears that had welled up. A sense of finality washed over me as I took one last look around the studio. The pain of losing Michael would never go away, but I could feel something shifting—a readiness to move forward. Maybe not tomorrow, but someday.

The phone rang, jolting me from my thoughts. It was Dash.

"Hey, Mom! Taylor and I are on our way. We picked up cupcakes from SusieCakes. Got your favorite—Red Velvet."

"Yum, I can't wait," I said, wiping a tear from my cheek, trying to focus on the warmth in his voice instead of the sorrow that lingered.

I glanced around Michael's studio one last time, and for a brief moment, it felt like I wasn't alone. The air seemed to thicken, as if his presence still lingered in the room, watching over me. My body shivered and I found myself instinctively scanning the shadows. But no, it was just my mind playing tricks.

Still, I couldn't shake the strange sense that he was there with me, somehow.

As I turned to leave, a faint creak echoed from behind me. I froze, my hand hovering over the door handle, my heart skipping a beat. I listened intently, straining to hear any sound beyond the quiet hum of the empty cottage.

Silence.

I took a deep breath and opened the door, stepping out of the studio for what I knew would be the last time. I half expected Irvin Skaggs to come after me like a horror movie bogeyman that never died. It sent chills down my body.

Of all the horrible things Skaggs had done, the worse was tainting my memories of Michael. Seeing him in a photograph would remind me of Skaggs. But I wouldn't let him have that. I was certain that with enough time, only my happy memories of Michael would endure, not what that monster did. I had to remind myself that the nightmare was over. Skaggs was dead. Dash and I were safe. It would take time, but we were going to be okay.

THANK YOU FOR READING

If you enjoyed this book and want to stay updated on my latest releases, get exclusive insights, and receive sneak peeks, join my newsletter at www.alanpetersen.com/signup.

I hope the book was as thrilling for you to read as it was for me to write. Stories like this thrive on the feedback and support of readers like you.

If you enjoyed it, please consider leaving a rating and a review on Amazon. Your feedback helps me reach new readers.

Keep the pages turning!

Alan

ABOUT THE AUTHOR

Alan Petersen was born in Costa Rica and raised in both Costa Rica and Venezuela. He moved to Minnesota for college, where he met and married his college sweetheart. Today, they live in San Francisco, atop one of the city's famously steep streets, with their feisty Chihuahua.

Visit him online at **www.AlanPetersen.com**. You can also tune into his podcast, *Meet the Thriller Author*, where he interviews bestselling authors from the Mystery, Suspense, and Thriller genres. Notable guests include Dean Koontz, Lee Child, Freida McFadden, Walter Mosley, and many more. Discover these insightful conversations at **Thriller-Authors.com**.

Connect with Alan...

ALSO BY ALAN PETERSEN

Stand-alone Psychological Thrillers

The Basement

Imposter Syndrome

The Elijah Shaw-Alexandra Needham FBI Mystery Thriller Series

Gringo Gulch

The Past Never Dies

Always There

Under A Crimson Moon

The Pete Maddox Thriller Series

The Asset

She's Gone

Odd Jobs

Made in the USA
Las Vegas, NV
14 July 2025